SLEEPLESS
VANESSA ROSE

Printed in the United States of America

First Printing, August 18, 2025

https://www.facebook.com/groups/vanessaroseromancereads

Edited by Amanda Brown and Tamsyn L. Key

Cover Design by SWEET 15 DESIGNS LLC.

To all who have loved. To all who have lost, and to all who chose to love again.

To Anthony, Baylee, and Bri!

And I can't forget all of the baristas who provided me with plenty of fuel as I loitered in their lobby to write.

CHAPTER ONE

NAOMI

The screaming still echoed down the hall and beyond the walls of the house. Brad and Jessie were there, pulling Naomi from the bed, but her hysterics never ceased. Naomi could still feel the ice-cold embrace of Paul wrapped around her, sinking into her like a ghost. She had no idea what had happened. Everything had been fine when they went to bed, but now . . . now nothing would ever be okay again.

"Call nine-one-one!" Brad screamed out toward Jessie who had already made the call.

Jessie's voice was shaky as she described the scene and their location to the operator on the other end of the line. Naomi couldn't hear the words; all she knew was Jessie had made the call. Instead, Naomi's head swam, making her dizzy and off balanced as she continued to scream in horror, the chilling sound tearing at her throat until it ached.

"Naomi! Naomi! Let me get you out of here!" Brad yelled, trying to pull her from the bedroom. He had to be loud as well because otherwise she would never hear him over her own cries of terror. Everything was happening in slow motion. She couldn't hear, couldn't think, couldn't speak. All that remained was feeling, which was the thing she wanted least. Cold... hard... empty.

Somehow, Brad managed to get Naomi out of the bedroom, and Jessie snatched a robe to wrap around her friend's naked body. It wasn't normal for Naomi to sleep with clothes on. After all, she and Paul had been engaged to be married. Naomi was so deep in shock that she was no longer functioning on her own. Brad put her shoes on for her as Jessie wrapped her in the robe and did her best to tie the front closed. They spoke to her, but their words were muffled by the horror replaying over and over in Naomi's mind. Nothing mattered anymore.

In the distance, the sirens wailed, the piercing call growing louder as they got closer to the house. Some point after being dragged into the living room Naomi stopped screaming and now sat still, staring at nothing yet seeing him. His body, white and gray, was pale in a way she had never seen before. People said the dead looked like they were sleeping, but he didn't. An eerie nothingness had been left in place of the man she had given her heart and soul to. Her mind replayed the incident over and over like a twisted reel from a news station. Paul had been sore the night before, complaining a bit about the bruises and cuts he had sustained from the accident, but the doctors had assured them he had no serious injuries.

Brad jumped up from the couch and opened the door for the first responders. "She hasn't been able to tell us anything. He is back here in the bedroom. I believe he was, well, I think she woke up to him like that."

Another responder came over to Naomi. "Hi, sweetie. My name is Amber. Can you tell me who you are?"

Naomi didn't respond, and after another attempt to ask, Jessie answered for her. At least Naomi was starting to hear again. Her body began to grow cold and heavy as the initial terror settled into shock. "Her name is Naomi Crestwood."

"Okay, Naomi, I'm here to help. I'm going to take you to the hospital to be checked out. Can you stand for me?" the first responder asked.

Still Naomi said nothing. She didn't move or even look at the woman. Her vision focused into the distance yet saw at nothing at all.

When Naomi once again did not respond or make any motion to move, the first responder got a stretcher. With Jessie's help, they moved her onto the rolling bed, wheeled her out of the house, and lifted her into the back of one of the ambulances.

The other one was open, and Naomi looked up to see another stretcher coming out of her house, their house. It was Paul, his body covered so no one would be able to gawk at his corpse. Brad was talking to the first responders, giving what little information he had.

Naomi should have been talking to them, explaining things, but she couldn't. It wasn't like she had any answers for them. She had woken up to him like that. Brad knew about as much as she did.

"Naomi, I'm going to pack up a few things for you and will meet you at the hospital. I'm right behind you," Jessie said and then walked away from the back of the ambulance.

"She is being pretty unresponsive. I'm going to give her a sedative to help calm her down. Her blood pressure is through the roof, but I'm sure it's shock. Once we get her calmed down, I'm sure it will go back to normal," Amber said, talking to a man who was sitting in the back of the ambulance with them.

"Alright, let's get going. Naomi, my name is Jared. I'm here to help. Can you try to tell me who you are?" the other responder asked and was again met with no response.

Her name didn't matter. Nothing mattered. She felt the poke of a needle followed by a warm sensation flooding her, and before long, she was asleep.

It was raining the day they put Paul in the ground. Naomi couldn't help but find the irony in it. Not just because in the movies it always rained at funerals but also because she and Paul had always loved the rain. On more than one occasion they had danced and played in the rain. It was cleansing for the soul. Their first kiss had been in the rain. Their first time making love had been in the back of his old Honda during a massive storm. They had been stranded on the side of the road, and one thing led to another. It had been beautiful and magical. The perfect night. Through their whole relationship, rain had been a blessing for them. Most people hated the rain but not Paul and her.

Naomi's mind wasn't focused on the words the preacher had to say, nor did she watch as one by one people went up to the coffin to lay a flower on top of it. Paul had no need for flowers. His soul was already gone, and the shell within the wood box didn't care. Why did people put flowers on the dead only for them to die as well?

Naomi had never thought of that before, but somehow now it occurred to her just how ridiculous it was. Paul would have laughed. Maybe he was laughing from wherever he was. The procession of people and their flowers continued, covering the coffin before it would be lowered into the ground. Naomi didn't get up to put a flower on the box. Her thoughts were focused on memories of Paul.

In truth, Naomi had felt nothing but numbness since being dragged out of their house. Jessie hadn't let her go back home, instead all of the planning and visits had taken place at Brad and Jessie's house, which was conveniently across the street. The four of them had done their best to get houses close to each other so they would be together forever, and their children would grow up together. That beautiful future would never come to fruition.

Jessie and Brad had taken on most of the work of planning the funeral. Naomi hadn't wanted to put that burden on them since they had only been married for a few months, but Jessie insisted. At the hospital, the doctors had prescribed some sedatives to Naomi to keep her calm and help her sleep, but sleep never came. Even heavily medicated, she found herself staying up until exhaustion forced her to fall asleep. The naps never lasted long, either. She woke up repeatedly screaming and terrified. Her eyes burned and itched, strained from lack of rest.

When they had left for the funeral, Jessie had tried to give her another pill, but Naomi said she wanted to feel her emotions. She didn't want to be a zombie while she said good-bye to the love of her life. Until then, she hadn't even really cried. The drugs had kept her detached. She owed him a proper good-bye, and that wasn't going to happen if she was drugged.

She and Paul had spent the better part of ten years together, dating through high school and college. Paul had recently asked her to marry him, and they were knee deep in the planning process. All of that was pointless now.

"Naomi, would you like to say something?" Jessie said, patting Naomi's hand.

Naomi looked up and around at all of the gathered people. Paul's parents were sitting next to her crying. They had so many friends, and everyone had showed up to pay their respects, but Naomi could not find it in her to stand up and talk to them all. Instead, she stood and walked to the edge of the pop-up canopy that had been set up to protect everyone from the rain. The preacher put a hand on her shoulder, and she looked over to him as well. The slightest smile rose on the corner of her lips, and then she went running.

She raced through the graveyard as the rain poured down on her, washing away the pain as best it could. Each drop reminded her of Paul and his love. Through the rain he was with her. Her legs pumped below her as she moved toward the road. In a small area with trees and benches for people to gather and visit with their loved ones, Naomi slammed into one of the tree trunks before turning and looking up through the canopy of leaves. Then she pushed off and began to dance around. For a moment, Paul was there, and they were dancing.

"Naomi! What are you doing?" Jessie called out as she caught up with her.

Naomi rushed over to her friend and pulled her into a dance. "It's raining!"

"Yes, it's been raining all day. Why are you out in it?" Jessie asked, pushing some of the soaked hair out of Naomi's face.

"Paul loves the rain. We love the rain. Dance with me!" Naomi answered. As they danced and played, Naomi's pain slipped away for just a moment. In her mind, she could hear Paul telling her to dance with him, feel his hands on her as she moved. For a moment the world stopped, and she could feel.

After a few moments, the clouds parted, and a stream of light cast down from above. Naomi looked up at it, and without skipping a beat, all of the joy dissipated, the agony returning. She screamed and finally the tears began to flow. Her body buckled and she became limp in Jessie's arms. The two of them lowered to the ground, and Jessie comforted Naomi while she cried.

"It's not fair! Why did this happen?" Naomi screamed.

"I don't know, sweetie. I don't know. Look, I've got you. Don't worry. I've got you," Jessie said, rocking Naomi and petting her hair back.

Naomi wasn't sure what she would have done if Jessie hadn't been there for her. She was more than a friend. She was a sister. They didn't leave until everyone else was gone. Paul's parents were holding a wake at their house, which was where the guest had all gone, but Naomi didn't think she could handle a room full of people asking her how she was feeling and telling her how sorry they were for her loss.

Instead, Jessie took her home. After they were changed and dry, they curled up on the couch. "Okay, let's get our minds off of this for a bit. How about I put in *Redemption*? I know how much you love Damion Malcom. Maybe seeing him for a bit will help you feel better," Jessie suggested putting an old DVD from their college days into the DVD player.

She wasn't wrong. Damion was the only man Naomi ever said could take her away from Paul. Of course, that was silly fangirl talk.

"I don't know, but we can try," Naomi whispered. "It's worth a shot."

"Oh, shots, that is a good idea, too," Jessie said grabbing a couple of glasses and a bottle of vodka.

"I don't think I can have alcohol with the medicine you keep feeding me," Naomi answered. "But have a double for me."

"You don't have to tell me twice." Jessie laughed, pouring a drink and sitting down on the couch. She pulled Naomi into her to snuggle as the movie began to play. The warmth of her friend holding her comforted her deep down in her soul.

"Thank you, Jessie. I mean, really. I don't think I could have done any of this without you," Naomi said, her voice breaking as tears welled up in her eyes again.

"Always," Jessie answered. "Always."

CHAPTER TWO

NAOMI — 5 YEARS LATER

She sat in one of the plastic chairs she kept just outside of her RV for when she needed some sun. Naomi had sold, thrown away, or donated almost everything from her life with Paul. All she had left were a few photos and the engagement ring he had given her, which she wore on a chain around her neck.

She held it now, twirling it as the sun shone down from above. The diamond cast rainbows across the grass, which made her smile. In the distance, she could see a cloud of dust puffing up into the air and signaling someone was on their way down the drive to where she parked her mobile home. It was a small piece of land but kept her away from people.

Naomi stood up and placed her hand above her eyebrows to shield the sun and give her a better look at who was coming. She was dressed casually for the day, wearing jeans and a white tank top, with her brown hair pulled up in a high ponytail to keep it out of her face. The sun had deepened her olive skin, and she was happy that the weather had finally warmed up after a very cold winter.

The blue sedan finally reached her and came to a stop before Jessie stepped out. Her curly red hair had enough product in it to kill a cow, but it made her curls flow perfectly. Naomi had always envied Jessie's hair, though she was glad not to have the freckled pale skin that came with it. Jessie always burned in the sun.

She had her green eyes covered by designer sunglasses her boss had gotten her the summer before and was dressed in a high-end pant suit, again the perks of working for the rich. Jessie wasn't allowed to share who her boss was, but Naomi knew it was someone famous and rich. She had always hated that Jessie couldn't talk more about her high-end client, but Jessie was a professional, so Naomi didn't pry.

"Welp, it's official. I'm pregnant!" Jessie said walking over to Naomi. She threw her hands up in the air the slapped them down on her sides as if she was talking about the weather.

"Wait? What?" Naomi asked, shocked at the nonchalant attitude her friend had when delivering the news. Joy swelled inside Naomi's chest, and she rushed over to wrap her arms around her friend.

"Well, I have been thinking for a couple of weeks now that I might be. Today I went to the doctor, and he confirmed, there is a grade A bun in this oven, baking away," Jessie answered.

The two of them squealed with glee and jumped up and down in excitement. Jessie and Brad had been trying for three years to get pregnant but had been struggling. They had even talked about seeing a specialist, but Jessie wanted to give it another year before resorting to the high-cost option. "Does Brad know yet?"

"Oh, he can wait in suspense a little while longer. I wanted to tell you first. After all, I've known you longer," Jessie teased, moving to the sitting area and taking a seat. She placed a hand over her stomach in that protective way all expectant parents did, and Naomi couldn't help but smile.

Naomi was ecstatic at the news that their little family was going to grow, but part of her ached, knowing the same would never happen for her dream of a family. "Do you want me to get you something to eat or drink?"

"Water. Anything else will make me throw up. To tell you the truth, I'm surprised Brad hasn't figured it out yet. Of course, men can be dense like that." Jessie laughed.

Naomi went inside and got them both some ice water before coming back to sit with her friend. While the days had gotten easier, and they were able to laugh, the sadness still lingered deep in Naomi's soul. She wasn't sure there would ever be a day she didn't think about Paul. There certainly weren't any nights. She had been so plagued with nightmares that most nights she didn't sleep. When she did manage to get some shut-eye, she wouldn't stay that way long, waking up in a panic and covered in sweat.

Jessie and Brad had been with her for a long time, letting her stay in their home, but eventually she had to move on and let them have their family. Part of the reason she lived so far from anyone else was so her screams wouldn't alert anyone. The idea of strangers running over to find out why she sounded like she was being murdered mortified her. No one would understand, and the longer the sleep deprivation went on, the worse it got. The vicious cycle was slowly killing her. Maybe that was exactly what she wanted.

"Yeah, men don't seem to notice that stuff most of the time, even ones as smart as Brad," Naomi answered, kicking her feet up on an old cooler she used as a table most of the time. They had all gone to college together. Naomi, Jessie, and Paul had gone into culinary and nutrition while Brad traveled the business path. The boring path, but he was good at it.

"Oh, don't go telling him that or he'll get a big head. Then I will never get him to do anything." Jessie giggled. She slowly sipped on the water and leaned back to soak in some of the sun. Already a tinge of pink was starting to form, and Naomi knew if she stayed there too long it would be lobster season.

"Well, you know you can't stick around here too long. He is going to want to know," Naomi said. It wasn't unusual for Jessie to come out and see her, but if she hadn't been feeling well, Brad would be more concerned if she was late. They were all a little tense at the idea of car wrecks after what happened to Paul.

"Yes, and I am going there as soon as I leave here. However, I wanted to ask you about something before I go home," Jessie said.

"Well, you already know I'm more than happy to be godmother, so there is no need to ask," Naomi said, laughing.

"Yes, and I wasn't going to ask that," Jessie said looking over to her friend and swatting her hand at her. "What I need to ask is if you might be my replacement at work. The doctor is already worried that since I had so many issues getting pregnant I might have trouble staying pregnant. He has already ordered me to pretty much stay off my feet and away from stress as much as possible. I was supposed to go on location for work, but that isn't happening. I told my employer I would find someone good, and you're the best."

"Oh, I get to finally find out who this super-secret employer is?" Naomi teased, leaning forward and putting her elbows on her knees.

"Only if you pass the interview process, but I already told him you are my first choice. Now listen to me, Naomi. He is very picky," Jessie explained. "I set you up a meeting with his assistant. If she likes you, she will schedule a tasting with the client."

"You set it up before you asked me? Jessie, I don't know if I want to go back to cooking," Naomi said, her tone turning sour. Along with giving up all of their personal items, Naomi had also sold the business she and Paul had been building up. They did food prep menus and cooking for people trying to stick to a healthy and clean diet. While they didn't believe in fad diets, they did make food that would nourish and strengthen anyone, and things had boomed for them.

"Naomi, look, it's been five years. You can't keep living like this. Take this as an opportunity to get out of this town and away from all the memories around here. You need to do something, and you really are the best," Jessie said, reaching over and taking Naomi's hand. "I really believe in you."

Naomi wasn't even sure what to say. Jessie had a point. She needed to move on, and after five years, she was still holding on to the past. Maybe she should take Jessie up on her offer. A new job out of town might be the perfect way for her to finally take a step or two forward and out of the darkness. However, with her history, there was the worry it would have the opposite effect.

"Go to the interview. If it isn't for you, you don't have to take the job," Jessie whispered, squeezing Naomi's hand.

"Okay, I'll give it a shot. You're right. I do need to get out of here. Besides, you said no stress, so if me taking your spot will take away some of your stress, it will be worth it," Naomi answered. She got up from her chair and went to give Jessie a hug. "I love you, and I'm so happy for you."

"Thank you. I know things aren't going to be easy, but I have such a wonderful support network." They hugged a little longer before Jessie started to make her way to her car. "Okay, I will send you the details. Bring your A game! I'm counting on you."

Naomi smiled, watching Jessie get into her car and drive away. She couldn't believe how much had changed, yet everything with her had stayed the same. Lifting the ring from below her shirt, she twisted it in the shine of the sun again. Paul would have wanted her to be happy. Turning, she went back into her RV. She would need to practice and get her bearings about her before her interview. At least it would give her something to do when she couldn't sleep. That had to be better than wallowing in her ever-present sadness.

CHAPTER THREE

NAOMI

Her heart was racing as she waited at the table for her interview to start. The point of contact for this job was Maria Donovan, and she had set them up at a small kitchen close to home. Well, near Jessie's home since Naomi lived too far outside of town for a restaurant to be anywhere near her. Everything was ready. She just needed Maria to show up.

"Sorry I'm late. I got caught up on another phone call. Thank you for meeting me. Jessie has said nothing but good things about you," a woman said.

Naomi assumed she was Maria since she was the only person who came into the restaurant. The woman was short, with a mess of brown curls framing her round face. She dressed in a pant suit that was a little tight and made Naomi curious as to why she hadn't had it tailored. All of Jessie's clothes fit her so perfectly that it seemed odd for the client's assistant not to be just as put-together. However, none of that stopped Maria from being a lovely woman.

"It's fine. Thank you for considering me," Naomi said, standing and reaching out to give the woman a handshake.

"Of course. We are so happy for Jessie. We know she has been trying to have a baby for some time," Maria said. "Now, I've been looking over your résumé, and it looks like you haven't worked in the food industry in several years. Can I ask why you stopped?" Maria asked, taking a seat at the table.

Naomi would have thought Jessie had filled her in on Naomi's past, but apparently she hadn't. Forcing a smile, she did her best to answer without breaking down. "I had some family things happen, and I stepped away from it for a while, but I have kept up with my education and practicing. I was never sure if one day I would get back into it."

"Education? So, you aren't just a chef?" Maria asked, looking up from Jessie's résumé.

"No, I'm also a nutritionist. It was my major focus of study, though I did get a full culinary degree as well. Jessie and I went to school together and graduated together. I just took extra classes," Naomi answered.

"Oh, well that is nice. I'm sure my client will enjoy that. He has been really focused on his health lately," Maria answered. "I know we sent over his specific dietary needs and expectations, so I'm ready for a tasting if you are. You will cook three meals a day plus snacks upon request."

"Yes, I have already started some things and have a full day's worth ready for you," Naomi answered.

She got up from the table and headed to the back of the restaurant. First, she brought out the breakfast and lunch she had prepared. Both were simple meals as the requested diet was pretty straightforward. Naomi waited while Maria tasted everything and then went back to get a few of the snack options and the dinner. "I have created all of these meals within the guidelines you sent over. They were very specific."

"What are these?" Maria asked picking up one of the biscuits that had been brought out with the breakfast plate.

"They are biscuits. They are made with whole grains and are high in fiber. With this low carbohydrate, added fiber is healthy for digestion," Naomi answered.

"Well, I'm not sure he will eat them, but I am finding them very tasty. Hey, do you mind to step outside for a bit?" Maria asked.

Naomi wasn't sure why the woman had made the request, but she smiled then stepped out front. She couldn't stop tapping her feet and playing with the corner of her shirt. The nervous habit had followed her from childhood. Naomi had never thought to work for someone else. She and Paul had always planned to open their own business. Things didn't work out that way, though, and now she got the joy of suffering through some nerve-racking job interviews. This one was worse, though, as it was the first position in her field since Paul had passed.

It had to have been ten minutes before Maria came to get her. When they got back into restaurant, Naomi started to clean up. Again, she was just trying to keep busy to appease her nerves. "So, did you like everything?"

"Naomi, I won't lie. Jessie was right about you. You are one hell of a cook. I'm not sure what he is going to think, but I did give him a call. He would like to meet with you tomorrow. Would you be available?" Maria asked.

"Yeah, I can come back. Will I need to prepare a whole menu again?" Naomi asked.

"No, just a dinner. He will want time to enjoy it. Oh, I have some paperwork I will need you to sign. I'm sure Jessie has told you about how things need to remain very private. It is important that you not tell anyone who you are working for. It keeps things easier for everyone. Trust me. You don't want my life," Maria said grabbing her brief case and pulling out a couple of sheets of paper. "These are standard forms. An NDA is required for anyone who works for him."

"Can I ask, who am I going to be working for? I would hate for you to go through all of this, and I end up not wanting to work for him," Naomi asked, pulling the papers to herself to look over.

"Sign the papers first. You will meet him tomorrow. If the two of you don't click, that's fine. We will find someone else," Maria answered.

Naomi took her time reading over the paperwork. None of it mentioned who she would be working for, instead it referred to him as "The Client." "Very well then. Let me read these over."

She took her time reading everything before signing each one. In truth, the mystery of it all made her want to continue. If things had been different, she would have probably turned the job down because of it. She hated not knowing who she would be working for, but this time, it was exciting. With a smile, she handed the paperwork back to Maria.

"Thank you. We can meet here again tomorrow at ten if that works for you. My client has other meetings later in the day, so won't be available for long. Make sure to have everything ready," Maria instructed. "See you tomorrow."

"See ya," Naomi said then went about cleaning up her mess. A good bit of food was still left, as cooking for one person was difficult. So, Naomi boxed up the leftovers to take over to Jessie's. With her morning sickness, she hadn't been too keen on cooking dinner, and Brad was having to work extra since Jessie was on bed rest. If nothing else, Naomi could give her friend a good meal or two to tide him over.

Jessie ran to the bathroom the moment Naomi walked in the room, leaving her and Brad in the living room.

"Well, I didn't mean to scare her off, but here. I cooked this stuff for my interview. It's a good bit of food, and I figured you might need some help."

Brad smiled, taking the bags. His dirty blond hair was a bit disheveled, and his brown eyes looked weary. Naomi had the feeling this was just the beginning of the man's sleepless nights. "I appreciate this. Jessie really isn't up for food these days, and I have been trying to keep the smell of it out of the house. I can take this to work, though, and eat there."

"How's she doing?" Naomi asked.

"I'm fine! Nothing to see here. I'm just in that lovely food and smells hate me phase. How did the interview go?" Jessie said, walking back into the room and plopping down on the couch.

If Naomi had thought Brad looked tired, Jessie looked exhausted. She was dressed in oversized sweats and her curls were pulled up in a messy bun.

"It went well. I have a second interview tomorrow," Naomi answered.

"Oh, that's great! Hey, promise me when you meet him, you won't act like an idiot," Jessie said, taking a few sips of water.

"Why would I do that?" Naomi asked. She was getting more curious than before.

"Trust me and promise me," Jessie added.

"The suspense is going to kill me. Tell me, please," Naomi begged, moving in closer to her friend.

"I can't. Rules are rules," Jessie said. She leaned her head against Naomi's shoulder. "Don't be nervous, though. He can be a bit of an asshole, but it's just his shield. Deep down, he's a big ol' softy. I really think you are going to like him."

"I see you intend to keep teasing me." Naomi laughed.

"Yep, and I'm getting the biggest kick out of it," Jessie answered.

Chapter Four

Damion

Nothing was going according to plan. Sure, he was happy for Jessie, but when he had signed on for this movie, he had his staff in place. Everything was set and perfect. Now he was having to make adjustments. It wasn't something he was excited to do. He was a creature of habit, most of the time. His schedule was packed with meetings as he got ready for the movie. They would be on location in some national forest in Georgia for several months, and then there would be the press tour, which often took him all over the world.

No, he didn't blame Jessie for abandoning him, but the last thing he wanted to do was start over with a new chef. Jessie knew how to cook for him. She understood him on a higher level, but with someone new, he would have to train them to his particular dietary needs.

Maria had secured a private location to avoid any unwanted run-ins with fans or the press. There was a reason he ensured everyone on his staff signed paperwork to keep them from talking about their connection to him. It not only protected his privacy but kept them from being harassed due to their relationship with him. Damion had chosen the life of a celebrity; his staff had only chosen to work for him. Maria was the only exception, as it was her job to get him auditions, interviews, and other work-related tasks.

"So, her name is Naomi. She has a degree in nutrition and culinary arts. Apparently, she went to school with Jessie and opened a meal prep business before shutting it down a few years ago," Maria said, going over everything in the prospects file as they drove to the restaurant.

"Why did she close her business?" Damion asked, taking the résumé and glancing over it. He wasn't really reading it as much as glancing as he listened to Maria talk.

"I didn't ask, and neither she nor Jessie provided any information. It was something to do with her family," Maria answered.

"Oh, okay. Well, I guess it doesn't matter. If she's good at her job, her past isn't any concern of mine," Damion said before pulling out a pack of cigarettes and lighting one up.

"You know those are going to impact your taste buds. The whole point of us being here is for you to taste the food," Maria said with a serious look.

"Yes, I am, which means this will be more accurate," Damion teased, taking a pull from the cigarette before letting out the smoke. He at least cracked the window to keep from filling the car with it.

"You are such an ass." Maria laughed. "Well, that is your call. Look, Damion. I know this is a lot to deal with, especially with the movie and you having to work with Allicia again, but give this girl a chance. I like her. Jessie likes her, so I think this might be your best shot."

Damion rolled his eyes. The last thing he was concerned about was working with Allicia again. He had worked with Allicia on several projects in the past, and they had great on-screen chemistry. Off screen was where it got complicated. They had made the typical mistake of taking their professional relationship private. While it never got serious, it had created a bit of tension between them. Damion was not the type of person to want anything serious, and she always wanted more than he was willing to give.

"Honestly, if you and Jessie like her, I'm probably going to go with it. I'm not really in the mood to do this."

"Well, sometimes even you have to adult. Okay, we're here. So put that thing out and let's get inside before anyone sees you," Maria said.

They had parked in the alley behind the restaurant to keep from being seen, not that anyone would expect him in the small-town Jessie was from. Sure, Atlanta wasn't too far away, so there was the probability that you could run into someone famous. Atlanta was starting to become the new Hollywood after all. It just wasn't likely to happen. Honestly, if he didn't have to be there, he wouldn't have come.

Once inside, Damion was met with the most pleasant aroma. It was savory and intoxicating which made his stomach growl with hunger he hadn't realized was there. He went from being indifferent about eating to starving in a matter of seconds. Maria led him down the hall to the dining room, but he almost turned directly into the kitchen from how hypnotizing the food smelled.

"I asked Naomi to just make dinner. I know that is the meal you care most about, even if half the time you don't eat it on set. Breakfast and lunch were good. She stuck to your request for the most part," Maria explained.

"What do you mean for the most part?" Damion asked, scrunching his face up.

"Well, I think she is going to reimagine how you see food," Maria answered in a matter-of-fact tone.

Damion wasn't sure what he thought about his assistant's answer. The last thing he wanted or needed as someone changing up his perfectly set routine. A table was already set for them with water and red wine. Damion couldn't hide his smile as he went to take a seat. This girl had really gone all out to make the interview showcase her skills.

"Okay, so in keeping with the provided information, I made steak in butter with a side salad and roasted broccoli. I set out a red..." the woman said coming out from the swinging door that led to the kitchen. However, she stopped talking once she looked up to see him. He wasn't at all surprised by the reaction but waited to see if she would recover before saying anything. "Umm, yes, I set out a red wine, cabernet sauvignon, to go with it. It pairs well with steak. I wasn't sure if you liked wine with dinner but thought I would give it a shot."

She recovered well. It was a point in her favor. He had people join his staff who could not manage working in close proximity to him. They couldn't separate their professional relationship with him from any fandom they also carried. It made things awkward, and he always ended up firing them. This girl seemed to shake off her shock and pick up with her work in only a matter of seconds.

The chef was not what he expected. She was pretty and well put-together, and her skin was sun kissed like she spent a lot of time outside. He liked that. However, he was curious about how tired she seemed. Her eyes were distant, and the dark circles under them suggested she hadn't slept in days. Damion figured she must have been nervous about the interview, though, so he put it out of his mind. Instead, he turned his focus back to the delicious meal he had been served that he couldn't wait to taste. "It smells wonderful. Thank you."

"Of course. Let me know if you need anything else. I will just be in the kitchen," the woman said. To her credit, she didn't completely run away, but he certainly noticed some shaking in her steps.

"Well, I think she handled that well," Damion said, picking up his silverware to cut into the steak. The food was perfectly cooked and well-seasoned. He was surprised at just how good it was. Maybe Jessie had given her some pointers or direction of how he liked things prepared. The meat almost melted in his mouth, and he moaned as he savored the taste of it all. What started out as a tasting turned into him devouring the whole meal.

"I'm going to say you liked it," Maria said, pushing her own plate away.

"I did, and she held her own. For a moment I wasn't sure," Damion answered.

"To her credit, she didn't know who you were going to be," Maria said.

The door to the kitchen opened, and Naomi walked back out. She had a towel in her hands and was wiping them as she made her way across the floor. "Well, what did you think?" Her tone remained professional, and the shock seemed to have worn off.

"Pretty good. I think you will do," Damion answered. He took a deep breath, not wanting to share with her just how much he enjoyed the meal. It had been the best steak he'd had in a long time. Even better than Jessie's, and he had never thought anyone could be better than Jessie.

"I will do?" Naomi asked and her eyebrow arched up just a bit.

"Look, I'm very particular about my food intake. I'm sure all of that information has been shared with you. Your cooking is good, and you come highly recommended. If you would like the position, it's yours. Maria can get you the details," Damion answered, standing up to leave. "Thank you for your time, but I have another meeting to get to."

He walked out and listened as Maria gave Naomi the rest of the information. When he reached the back door, he smiled. He really hoped she would take the job. Something in him said she was going to be good for him. It was just going to take time to get used to someone new.

CHAPTER FIVE

NAOMI

The amount of paperwork she had to read and sign was crazy, but she had a feeling it would be worth it. Naomi was lucky she had her own RV to take with her instead of having to pack up her stuff to still end up living in a trailer. The night before she left, she stayed with Jessie and Brad. She was in need of some time with them before she left to go to the filming location. Originally, they wanted to take her to dinner, but Jessie wasn't in the best position for eating. Instead, they decided to have a movie night with saltine crackers and ginger ale.

"I still can't believe that you have been working for Damion Malcom this whole time. How were you able to keep the secret?" Naomi said, tossing a cracker at her friend.

"Them's the rules," Jessie said in a silly voice before laughing as the cracker hit her in the chest and crumbled a bit. "I wasn't allowed to talk about it, and believe me, it was difficult. I knew how much you were a fan. Many times I just wanted to run to you."

"Yeah, I get it, but it's me! You know I never would have said anything," Naomi said.

"I couldn't risk it. This job has been so important to me, and I couldn't afford to lose it," Jessie said, picking up what was left of the cracker and chomping on it. "But I'm glad you know now. It will make things easier when I go back to work. Besides, I get to hear all of the gossip while I am stuck here with my feet up."

"True. Of course, I'm a little nervous about this. Remember I had his posters all over my walls when we were in high school. I hope I don't embarrass myself, acting like some sort of crazy fangirl. I swear I almost did when I was at the interview. I totally paused for a second and had to get my composure." Naomi laughed.

"Oh, I know. He called me as soon as he left and told me all about it. He likes you, but don't let him get away with being an asshole. He will push you. Especially if you push him about his diet," Jessie said with a stern look.

"So, treat him like a petulant child who won't eat their vegetables?" Naomi asked.

"Yeah, something like that, except it will be bread. You'll see, but I promise, he's a good guy deep down," Jessie answered.

The two of them laughed and threw on a movie, enjoying the night together. Naomi would be leaving first thing in the morning if not sooner. It all depended on whether she was able to sleep.

She sat straight up as a scream tore from her lips. It was just another reminder why she had moved so far away from town so people wouldn't hear her when she had her nightmares. They had never gone away, and she wasn't sure if they ever would. Checking her phone, she realized it had only been an hour since she lay down. Her body shaking, she got up and made her way to the front of the RV. No way would she be getting any sleep, so she decided to start her trip.

The movie was being shot in a very remote area of Georgia. When she put it in the GPS, it showed up as being in the middle of the Chattahoochee-Oconee National Forest. Naomi had already made a note of how far away any of the stores would be. She was going to have to stay on top of her supplies to avoid having to make unnecessary trips while at the same time keeping things fresh.

She pulled into the last shop on the way to the filming location. It wasn't open yet, so she just parked outside and waited. Getting what she needed for her first few days was going to help her be able to settle in more smoothly. While she waited, she made a pot of coffee and worked on the menu for the next few days. With that, she wrote up her shopping list. Maria had assured her she would have a decent kitchen trailer with adequate space for groceries. The trailer would be next to where she parked and near Damion's trailer to keep things centralized. Naomi couldn't wait to see the setup so she could figure out how her day-to-day would be.

Once the store opened, she got all of her shopping done, making sure to catalog the receipt like Maria had told her. She headed into the national forest to find the set. Security was posted all around the perimeter, and Naomi had to be shown where to go. She was given her badge and told to make sure to keep it on her at all times. Unsurprisingly, people were always trying to break into movie productions.

"Wow you got here a lot earlier than expected. Damion won't be in until tomorrow, so you have all of today to get yourself settled in. Let me show you to the kitchen," Maria said as Naomi flung open her door.

"I need to plug in my RV and get it set up," Naomi answered, looking around to make sure she was parked out of the way.

"We have people who can help you with that. They will be around shortly. Until then, let me show you around," Maria answered. "This building next to where you parked is the kitchen. It is for Damion only, so you won't have to worry with feeding a bunch of people. He will let you know if he is having anyone over, but between you and me, he never does. That trailer across from you is Damion's. Beyond this point there are a bunch of trailers for other crew members. Allicia is parked on the other side along with some of the other actors. Damion likes to be away from people."

"Should I move then?" Naomi asked, trying to make sure she was taking in all of the information.

"No, he will want you close by. Not to worry," Maria answered. "Okay, here is my place. You can bring me any invoices you have. Please make sure to log everything. It is very important. You should have already gotten a credit card for you to use for purchases as well. We don't want you having to use your own money to buy things. Oh, speaking of, you will get paid every week on Friday. Did you fill out your direct deposit form?"

"I did. It is in the packet of papers you had me fill out. I have it in my RV," Naomi answered.

"Good, get those to me by the end of the day so I can start processing everything," Maria said.

"I thought you were just Damion's agent?" Naomi said, her voice coming out more like a question than a statement.

"Oh, I'm Damion's everything. I have been working with him for the better part of seven years now, ever since he really took off. Sure, he was popular when he was younger. Teeny boppers and all, but he has come a long way since that," Maria answered.

"That sounds like a lot of work," Naomi said. She was impressed with how much the woman had to take care of.

"It is, and I'm paid well for it. One day, I will be able to retire in style, but for now, I'm working hard. It makes me happy," Maria replied. "Alright, I will get some people over to help you get things set up. Here are the keys for the kitchen, so you can start making it yours. I will let you know when Damion is coming so you can be ready to start. Until then, enjoy the beauty of nature. This is by far one of the nicest sets I've ever been to."

Naomi took the set of keys and clicked them onto the lanyard her badge was on. She waited at her RV to give instructions on what needed to be done. Once the team was working on her RV, she went to set up the kitchen. It was nice enough, considering it was in a mobile building. She stocked the fridge, checked out the pots and pans, and made a note of anything she might want to add. For the most part, it had everything. It was probably how Jessie had it set up, but she would want to add a few things for her preference.

"Oh, Paul, I think if you could see me now, you would be proud of me. This isn't going to be easy, but I'm finally trying. I know I need to," Naomi whispered, feeling her heart ache at the thought of her late fiancé.

CHAPTER SIX

NAOMI

O n her first official day of work, Naomi had woken up at three
in the morning from another nightmare. She had managed to
get about two hours of sleep before she was too shaken to try and
fall asleep again. So she decided to go on and prep for work. Turning
on some good music, Naomi danced around the kitchen while she
gathered ingredients and started her *mise en place*. For her first day, she
wanted to really show her worth. Dinner was going to be a slow cooked
pot roast with carrots, green beans, and mushrooms. Lunch would
consist of a turkey and vegetable wrap that would easily travel to set.
She would pair it with some berries and a green smoothie. Damion was
"low carb," but she knew that a healthy diet required carbs. No way
was she going to let someone under her care fall victim to fad diets.

Once dinner and lunch were prepped, she started on breakfast.
She planned to make a vegetable frittata with apples on the side and
a biscuit. Sure, she knew she would be pushing buttons by making
them, but they were full of fiber and whole grains. Unlike traditional
biscuits, these were modified to fit a healthy diet. If he didn't eat it, he

would still have a very filling breakfast, but she wanted to see what she could get away with.

She was surprised that by the time she finished getting everything prepped and started, the sun had already risen. Maria had informed her Damion woke up early and went on a run. He would prefer to eat breakfast by six so he could be on set by eight at the latest. With everything prepped, she was ready to start breakfast to have it fresh for him when he finished his run. It certainly worked out for her that she didn't sleep a lot. She was plating his food when she heard the door to the building open. She immediately headed out to set the plates on the table. Already there was a glass of water, a glass of fresh-squeezed orange juice, and a carafe of coffee.

Damion moved to sit down at the table, pushing his sweaty hair away from his face. He was flush and breathing heavily, and Naomi felt heat rising on her cheeks. It still shocked her that she was working for one of her favorite actors of all time.

"What is this?" Damion asked, poking the biscuit with his fork.

"What does it look like?" Naomi countered, a smile curling on her lips as she raised an eyebrow.

"It looks like carbs. I don't do carbs," Damion answered, sitting back and looking at her. He had a defiant look that she couldn't help but find sexy. "Why did you even bother?"

"Well, you do 'do carbs' as you say. Vegetables and fruit all are carbs. So, saying you don't do them is a misnomer. Also, they are important for your health. They fuel your body for long days on movie sets as well as ensure your brain is functioning at full capacity," Naomi answered, crossing her arms over her chest.

"I've been doing just fine without them. You can take it away now," Damion grumbled, turning to the rest of his breakfast.

"They also help you poop," Naomi added and then turned to go back into the kitchen. She didn't wait for him to respond, but she could feel him glaring at her the whole time she walked away.

Part of her thought to ask about him eating alone. It seemed sad, but coming from someone who ate alone all the time, she thought he might find it peaceful. So instead, she turned down the music and went about cleaning up the kitchen. One of the difficult things about cooking for just one person was there would always be leftovers. Not wanting them to go to waste, she made herself a plate and one for Maria as well.

Once breakfast was packed up, Naomi made Damion's lunch and put it away. She wasn't sure if she was supposed to send it with him after breakfast or deliver it later in the day. It was added to her list of questions for Maria. The list helped her stay organized. That way she wouldn't forget.

With the kitchen in order, she went out to the dining area to collect Damion's plates. He had eaten everything except for the biscuit, which made Naomi laugh. He hadn't seemed angry, just mildly annoyed, so she had decided that was the hill she was dying on. She would offer him biscuits until he gave in.

With Damion's dishes, she finished off the cleaning and made sure the roast was set to the lowest setting to ensure it would be as tender as possible. Then she went in search of Maria. She was in her trailer sitting at a desk and talking on the phone. It was awe-inspiring to watch the woman work. Nothing seemed to bother her as she talked, working on some sort of negotiation or deal for Damion. Naomi couldn't tell what it was, but she waited for Maria to acknowledge her before saying anything.

"Hey! So, I heard you offered Damion a biscuit," Maria said, a hint of laughter in her voice.

"Yeah, well, not just any biscuit. These are actually made with health in mind. I can't help it if he likes to be foggy-headed and unable to poop right," Naomi answered passing a box over to Maria.

The woman took the box of food and burst out laughing. "Yeah, he told me you said that too. I have to say, you are everything Jessie said you would be. She has been fighting with Damion about his diet for years."

"Well, he's getting older. It's harder to keep up proper brain function as we get older," Naomi answered.

Maria motioned for her to take a seat and join her for a bit, so Naomi sat down in the other chair. "Don't let him hear you say that. He is trying too hard to pretend that he's still twenty."

"Well, I don't think I would like him as much if he were. I mean, I loved him when he was twenty, but I think he is more handsome now," Naomi admitted, knowing she was blushing.

"Yeah, Jessie told me you were a bit of a fan. I have to say, you're holding it together a lot better than I thought you would. I'm glad you are able to stay professional. I have worked with him for so long he is more like an annoying child than anything else," Maria said. She took a bite of breakfast and made the loudest most inappropriate sounding moan Naomi had ever heard. The woman was obviously enjoying her meal. "Okay, I am going to marry you now."

Naomi burst out laughing. She honestly felt so out of practice she was worried her food wouldn't be as good. "Well, you might should take me to dinner first."

"Deal, done! There is no way I'm letting you out of my life now. This is the best damn breakfast I have had in my entire life!" Maria responded and then went back to enjoying her meal.

"Well, let's see what happens. You aren't really my type," Naomi answered, laughing. "Oh, Maria, I do have a couple of questions if you have a few moments."

"Once I finish this foodgasm I will be all yours," Maria teased. "Okay, what ya got for me?"

"Well, with lunch, do I deliver it to him, or do I send him with a lunch box like a schoolboy?" Naomi asked first.

"Oh, I will usually deliver it, but if you want to take it, you can. I can show you when and how. Lunch time is hit and miss with filming. It all just depends on how things are going," Maria answered.

"Yeah, just let me know when you are heading over, and I will meet up with you so I can learn the ropes. The next question I have is if it's okay for me to run into town to get a few more things for the kitchen. I like to have a better scale for weighing ingredients and I prefer a few other types of utensils when cooking professionally."

"Yes, get anything you need. Just make sure to log your receipts like I showed you. The card you have doesn't have a limit, but of course, be within reason. If you are getting something over five hundred, drop me a line for approval," Maria explained. "We want you to have everything you need."

"Perfect. I will go tomorrow after breakfast, so I have plenty of time. I will just have his lunch in the fridge ready to go," Naomi said.

"Looking forward to it. I will get with you to deliver lunch today, so you have an idea of how to do it in case I'm not here or you just get curious about how things work on a movie set. Jessie started to get bored with going after a while, so I started taking it. I always have a midday meeting with Damion anyway," Maria said.

CHAPTER SEVEN

DAMION

H e wasn't sure if he should be irritated or amused by Naomi's little push about breakfast. She was smart and funny, not to mention very pretty. No, she didn't have the commanding presence of a starlet like his costar Allicia, but something about her made Damion think what it would be like to be closer to her. Not that he was looking for a relationship, nor was it a good idea to get involved with an employee. No, she was just interesting, and he wanted to learn more about her.

When he had finished his shower and started to head to the set, he had seen her going into Maria's trailer. She had been carrying a little to-go box, and Damion smiled realizing that his new chef was going to take care of Maria too. It wasn't required, but he appreciated it. Maria worked too hard not to be treated well.

After that, his day officially started. He was sent to hair and makeup right off the bat. Allicia was already there being painted for her role. They weren't doing anything too pronounced as the movie was set in the middle of nowhere. However, sometimes it took more makeup to make you look like you weren't wearing any but still cover any flaws. Allicia had a scar on her chin, which she insisted had to be covered in every movie she was in. It was something the woman hated about herself, and Damion had never understood why. It wasn't large, and it made her look more normal. Once he had tried to convince her that it made her special, but she wasn't hearing it.

"I hear you got a new chef. What happened to the last one?" Allicia asked, looking up from her phone.

The woman was beautiful. She had almost black hair, which had been pulled back while her makeup was being done. Her eyes were a deep green and her nearly flawless skin had a light pink tone to it. She was a little tall, but not by much. It made her a good match for him since he was very tall. Allicia also had curves in all the right places, something Damion had gotten acquainted with in the past.

"She is having a baby so couldn't come on location. The new girl was recommended by Jessie, and I think she is going to do well. Her food is excellent," Damion answered. Breakfast had been better than expected, even with the little argument over bread and what carbs were. He had been pleasantly surprised and hoped that the meals stayed on that level.

"Good, I'm glad you were able to find someone else who works well for you. I know how picky you can be," Allicia answered, but she'd already turned back to her phone. A lull of silence passed between them before Allicia spoke again. "So, I was thinking, when we work together people like to talk. This is what, our fourth movie together. Maybe we should play that up on social media."

"Allicia, I really don't want to go down that road again." Damion groaned. They had dated in the past. They made romance movies together, and sometimes it was difficult to separate the emotions on and off the screen. It had been a huge mistake—one he had no intention of repeating.

"Why? We make a good couple, and we aren't getting any younger. People are going to start wanting to see us settling down some. Besides, don't we always have fun together?" Allicia pushed.

"Yes, we have fun, but I'm not looking to settle down. I have no desire to tie myself to anyone. My life is fine the way it is," Damion answered.

"Miss, we are done with your makeup. We need to move you to wardrobe," the makeup artist said, interrupting the conversation.

"Just think about it, Damion. It might be better than you think," Allicia said in a huff as she pushed out of the chair and left the trailer.

"She is never going to give up," Abby, Damion's makeup and hair artist said with a sigh.

They had been working together for a long time, and even though the girl was ten years younger than him, she had already made a name for herself in the industry. She was medium height, and her slim body lacked curves. Her hair was purple at the moment and framed her face in a cascade of curls that landed on her shoulder. Damion had always loved just how vibrant her blue eyes were and often found himself staring at them when she was working on his face—not in a romantic way, just an appreciation of beauty.

"Allicia? Yeah, she will. She'll get tired of me being the normal me and give up. She did the last time we worked together," Damion answered.

Abby moved behind him and started looking at his hair. She often would check for dead ends or sign of it needing a trim. Filming movies could take months, but as with the case of the one he was filming now, the film was only set in a few days. His hair couldn't change too much during the process. "Okay, I think you are good, but you will need a trim in a couple of weeks. I'm going to make a note. Also, I'm going to give you some leave-in to use. Your hair needs protection with all the heat beating down on it regularly. Make sure you use it after each wash."

"Sure, I can do that," Damion answered. "Anything else?"

"No, not yet, but I'll let you know. You're pretty good at taking care of yourself," Abby answered. "I'll see you in a bit. I'm sure you are ready for a smoke before wardrobe."

"Oh, you know me so well," Damion answered, getting up from the chair. He had just stepped out of the trailer when he saw Maria and Naomi walking up. They didn't seem to have noticed him as Maria was showing Naomi around.

Damion lit up a cigarette and made his way over to them, "What do you think?"

Naomi jumped a bit, and Damion couldn't help but chuckle. Maria swatted at him and shook her head. "You really shouldn't sneak up on people like that. It's the girl's first day. You're going to scare her off."

"Sorry, but still, what do you think of all of this?" Damion was still laughing as he asked his question again.

"It's all a bit much. I'm not sure I will ever get used to it, but it is interesting. How was breakfast? You left before I could ask," Naomi said, looking around. Her eyes were wide in wonder, and part of him just wanted to show her around and give her the details of the business. Maria was doing that, but it wasn't the same.

"Breakfast was very good. Thank you," Damion answered.

"You know, for someone so focused on your health, you sure are doing something horrible for it," Naomi said, pointing to his cigarette.

"Well, we all have our vices. At least I know what's going to take me out," Damion teased.

For a brief moment, Naomi's eyes looked sad and distant. Her skin grew a little pale, and she swallowed hard. It only lasted a moment and was gone just as quickly as it showed up. Something about what he said had gotten to her. He started to ask about it but thought better of it.

"Well, there are better ways to go out," Maria said. "I've been trying to get him to quit for years."

"It's hard. I've been smoking since I was a teen. I started because of a movie I was in, and I just never put it down," Damion admitted.

There were worse things for him to get into when being in the business. So far, he had managed to keep from being taken away by drugs. Sure, he drank, but not so much that it hurt him. His biggest vices were smoking and women—two things that didn't really hurt him in the long run.

"That's a long time to be smoking. I can't believe they let you smoke that young," Naomi said. She was so naïve, and it made him smile.

"Well, it is what it is. I could be doing worse, so I don't think much about it. Oh, by the way, Maria, I have a list of a few things I need from town. I forgot to get them before I came in," Damion said, remembering he was running low on cigarettes.

"I'm already going to town. Do you just want me to get it while I'm out?" Naomi offered. "I was going to wait and go tomorrow, but I can go today. Dinner is already cooking and doesn't need my attention."

Maria looked from her toward Damion, and he gave a nod, "If you want. I will make notes, so you get the right stuff. Maria knows my preferences, but I'm sure you can handle it."

"I've been to the store before. I'll be fine," Naomi answered.

They walked over to a table, and Damion took Maria's notebook to make a list with details to give to Naomi. It would be interesting to see what she pushed him with after going shopping. "You can call Maria if you have any questions. I have to go. They are going to need me on set soon."

"Sure, I'll get right on this," Naomi answered.

He started to walk away but then turned and winked at the ladies. While he was still apprehensive to have someone new on his team, he was really starting to like Naomi.

CHAPTER EIGHT

NAOMI

She managed to make it back from the store with plenty of time to get dinner finished. The items Damion had requested sat in a bag on the counter opposite where she was cooking. The list hadn't been long, but she certainly felt odd buying cigarettes. She had never been a fan, even when some of her other classmates had started to pick up the habit. Damion had requested two cartons of the things along with mints, gum, toothpaste, and a very specific cologne. It took her a while to find the last item, but she managed, especially since she was already at the mall to get the stuff she needed for her kitchen.

Damion's plate had just been finished when he peeked back into the kitchen. "Hey, Naomi. I'm not staying for dinner tonight. Sorry, I should have said something earlier, but I'm going out tonight. Did you get that stuff for me?"

"Yes, I did. That isn't a problem. Do you want me to save it for your lunch tomorrow, or maybe for later?" she asked, grabbing the bag and handing it over to Damion.

"No, you can give it to Maria or have it for yourself. I'll be out late, and there isn't really a place to heat up leftovers on set. Thanks for understanding," Damion answered and left before she had a chance to say anything else.

"Okay then, I'll just take some to Maria," Naomi said to no one. With a deep sigh, she packed up the meal and put one serving in the fridge for her own lunch the next day. She split the rest of the meal up into another serving for herself and a serving for Maria to have for dinner.

When she got to Maria's trailer, she once again tapped on the door. "Hey, I'm kinda busy tonight. Did you bring me dinner?" the woman asked.

"Yes, I did. Try to eat something," Naomi encouraged, handing over the box.

"Thank you, and I mean it. Are you alright after your first day?" Maria asked, even though she wore had a rushed look.

"I'm fine. Just eat something when you can. Let me know if I can help with anything," Naomi answered with a smile.

"I will, thank you again," Maria answered. She went back into her trailer, and Naomi turned to go back to her RV.

She hadn't put a lot of thought into what she would do during her downtime. She had thought to be busier with Damion, but she found herself rather void of anything to do. The kitchen only took a few minutes to clean, and everything else was ready for her to start again in the morning. Looking at the time, she noticed it was only seven, which meant she had several hours before she had to start again.

With a sigh, she made her way to her RV and pulled a chair out in front. She pulled up the awning and set up an outdoor sitting area. A small mosquito trap hung from above and gave off a small blue glow. Once everything was set up, she grabbed a drink and took a seat. Pulling out her phone, she turned on a playlist she had made not long after Paul had died. It was a list of all the songs they had enjoyed and danced to when they were together—one of many things Jessie claimed she'd held on to for too long.

"Oh, Paul, Jessie is probably right. I should just let you go," Naomi whispered, but just saying the words brought a powerful ache to her heart. Tears formed in her eyes, and she couldn't stop a couple from leaking out.

"Now why are you crying?" a familiar voice asked. "You have nothing to cry about."

Naomi looked up and saw Paul there, standing before her. "You're here?"

She saw a sparkle in his blue eyes as he leaned down to stroke her cheek. Naomi lifted her hand to rest over his, but her hand touched only her own cheek. Paul wasn't really there, of course, even though she could see his short brown hair and the slight lines around his cheeks when he smiled. Naomi missed his smile almost as much as his touch. She missed everything about him.

"I wish you could stay with me. I feel so lost without you," Naomi whispered, laying her head back against her chair.

"I'm always with you, Naomi. Always," Paul answered. It was all in her head, but those moments, when she could conjure up his memory, were often the most peaceful moments of her day.

Softly, she started to sing along with the song playing out of her phone. She wasn't the best singer in the world, but she wasn't bad either. Once upon a time, she would sing in the kitchen while she and Paul cooked. Sometimes they would get distracted and dance around, and the whole ordeal would make her laugh. He was meant to be hers for the rest of her life, but that was never going to happen.

"Always," she whispered.

A crashing sound pulled her out of her fantasy, and she looked across the yard to see Damion stumbling into his trailer with a woman she had never seen before. It wasn't like she expected to recognize whoever he was involved with. However, watching them kiss and disappear into the trailer, she got the feeling this wasn't a very long acquainted situation. He seemed more interested in something physical, or maybe she was reading too much into it.

Naomi sat there for a while more before deciding to go back into her RV. Spying on Damion wasn't the best idea in the world, and she should try to get a little rest before waking up for work. After her first day, she had started to realize that being up early worked in her favor. By the time she finished her drink and showered, she could feel the pull of exhaustion taking over. However, as she lay down, the memories started again.

"I promise. I'm fine. I just need a little sleep," Paul said, pulling back the blanket and climbing into bed.

"Only if you're sure. I can get you more pain meds if you think you need them," Naomi said, looking at him from across the bed. They were both stripped down and ready for sleep after such a stressful day. The wreck had totaled his car, but he hadn't been badly injured, which was what mattered the most.

"It's just a bunch of scrapes and bruises. Nothing a good night's sleep won't fix," Paul answered.

He got into bed and moved in close, pulling Naomi into the circle of his arms. She sighed deeply, feeling warmth and safety. Nothing felt more like home than sleeping in Paul's arms. They had been together forever and would be getting married in the spring. She couldn't wait.

"I love you," Naomi whispered, closing her eyes.

"I will always love you," Paul responded.

Her heart started to race. Everything turned dark and tinted blue. Cold. All she could feel was the cold of ice surrounding her. She flung open her eyes, trying to figure out what had happened. How was she so cold? Nothing made sense. Paul. It was Paul. He was cold. Why was he cold?

Naomi screamed and sat straight up in her bed. Turning to see the clock, she had been asleep less than an hour. It was always the same. Her dreams started out so sweet and ended so horrific. Jumping out of bed, she went to grab a bottle of vodka. A few shots should calm her nerves and help her get back to sleep.

She pulled on her robe and went to sit outside. Maybe the cool fresh air would help relax her. It was a beautiful night, and she was surrounded by nature. How could that not be soothing? With one shot and then another, Naomi was able to find her breath. Across the yard, Damion's door flung open and the woman from earlier stepped out holding a few of her clothing items as if she couldn't be bothered to put them back on.

"So, I'll see you later?" the woman asked, leaning up for another kiss from Damion.

He smiled at her and returned the kiss. "Have a good night, April." His words didn't acknowledge the woman's request, and Naomi arched a brow in wonder.

As the woman made her way down the path to leave, Damion looked over at Naomi. She simply smiled and raised the bottle of vodka as if to toast to Damion's conquest. Then she took a swig from it. Damion just shook his head and went back into this trailer. She found it odd that he didn't even walk the woman to her car or to get a cab. It was like she had been ejected and forgotten just as quickly as she had been invited. What an asshole. Maybe it was best that they had a business relationship. She would hate to be on the receiving end of his romantic ones.

CHAPTER NINE

DAMION

They were already through with their second week of filming, and Damion found himself starting to get drained. It didn't help that Allicia was still bothering him to upgrade their relationship, if for no other reason the good publicity, but Damion knew better. If he started things up with Allicia again, she would want to push for more, and that wasn't something he was looking to get involved in.

"Will you be here for dinner tonight?" Naomi asked, coming out of the kitchen with his breakfast. Usually, she wore a smile, but Damion couldn't help but notice the frown. Her eyes were dark and bloodshot, and he wondered if it was the lack of sleep she was getting. He noticed her getting up early and had even heard her screams. Part of him wanted to ask why she had such horrible nightmares, but it wasn't really any of his business.

"No, I have a date tonight," Damion answered, watching her as she set the plates down on the table. Their usual playful banter didn't seem appropriate with the look on her face. He even noticed a hint of redness on her face that made him think she had been crying.

"Alright, then. I won't make any. I was going to make a trip to town today anyway, so that works out. I'll have Maria bring over your lunch later," Naomi answered as she set the smallest plate on the table. She had made these biscuits every day since they met. He wasn't sure why he gave her such a hard time over them. Jessie had told him she was a certified nutritionist, and he should trust her judgment, but he just had too much fun poking at her.

"You just don't give up. Do you?" he asked, testing the waters and poking at the small bread product.

"They are good for you, and I bet if you would try them, you would find you enjoy them too," Naomi answered, a slight turn of a smile showing on her lips.

"Maybe, but today is not that day," Damion answered, getting started on the omelet she had made him. He had to admit, she was a damn good cook. At least she was good at portions because if she offered him more, he would eat more. It was hard to resist.

"Suit yourself. You need me to get anything for you in town? Fiber supplements?" Naomi teased back and started to show signs of pulling out of whatever made her so sad.

Damion burst out laughing and leaned back in his chair some. "Keep this up, I might have to drag Jessie back from maternity leave. She doesn't give me so much lip."

"You wouldn't dare," Naomi said in mock offense.

"Oh, I would. I'm sure she could figure out how to cook with her feet up. I'll buy her one of those little kitchens they torture people with on those food challenge shows," he answered, leaning forward and staring Naomi right in the eyes.

"She will poison you if you do that to her. Trust me. Her red hair isn't just for looks. It's a warning sign," Naomi answered and turned to head back into the kitchen.

Something about making Naomi laugh made Damion feel better. They weren't really friends. The only time they spent together was during breakfast and sometimes dinner, though those were few and far between. He liked to keep himself busy after work. However, he had no doubt that if he spent more time with her, he could be friends with her. She had a good sense of humor and a little bit of fire in her. There certainly wasn't a lack of defiance, which she proved every day with the damn biscuits. He looked at the offensive baked good and poked it again.

He started to cut into it when the kitchen door opened again, and Naomi walked back into the room. Damion jumped back as if getting caught stealing cookies from a cookie jar. Heat rose on his cheeks, and he did everything he could to hide it.

"What's this? Were you giving in to the call of the dough?" Naomi teased, arching a brow at him.

"No, I was just playing with it," Damion protested, knowing he had been caught red-handed.

"Right... I will pretend to believe you," Naomi said laughing. She started to pick up some of the items off of the table but left the biscuit.

"Have fun in town today," Damion said, getting up to get ready for his day. It was going to be a long day, and he was not looking forward to it. Honestly, he would have loved to take a day off, but work came first, and they were on a strict filming schedule.

It had been raining since early afternoon. They shut down the afternoon shoot, and Damion was thankful for the early day. He was tired

and wanted a little rest. He had just gotten back to his trailer when he saw Naomi by the kitchen unloading her car. Usually, he would go over to help, but she had that look again. Something was bothering her, and he wasn't sure he was ready to get that personal with his chef.

Instead, he went into his trailer and flopped down on his bed. It was a comfortable bed, even though the room as a whole was on the small side. Reaching into his pocket, he pulled out his pack of cigarettes and lit one up before grabbing his phone to let his date know that he would be ready earlier than expected.

Since the day ended early, he decided to go out a little earlier too. He hadn't even had lunch yet, but an early dinner just meant more time for post-dinner activities. Julia, his date for the night, was very pretty, and he had no doubt she would show him a good time. Damn he sounded like an asshole, even to himself, but she was the one who offered.

A loud knock sounded on his door, and he got up to see who it was. "The rain had me coming back earlier than expected. I didn't want to be driving in it. Maria said you didn't get your lunch yet, so I wanted to drop it off to you," Naomi said from the other side of the door.

Damion took the cigarette out of his mouth and blew the smoke away from her, remembering how much it bothered her. "Thanks, I'm actually going to an earlier dinner since my day got cut short."

"Well, maybe have some of it to tide you over. I wouldn't want you to get over hungry. You are on a bit of a schedule," Naomi insisted, moving the plate closer to him.

"I'm not a baby," Damion teased, arching a brow at her. "But I do appreciate it. I'll put it in my fridge. Right now, I think I want a nap. You look like you could use one too."

"I'm fine. I still have some stuff I want to do. Have fun on your date tonight," Naomi answered, turning to walk across the yard to her RV.

She was soaked by the time she got there, but it didn't seem to bother her. Of course, she was wearing jeans and a white T-shirt, which meant he got a very clear view of her body. The fabric clung to her and was see through in places. At that moment, he forgot she was his chef, and something else started to stir inside of him. With a deep breath, he pushed it down. Naomi was his employee, not a person of interest in the dating department.

It took him a few moments more to finish his cigarette, and then he could get a nap. He wanted to be well-rested for his night.

Chapter Ten

Naomi

Storms were always the hardest. One of the first times she and Paul had ever danced together was after school one day when a storm was pelting the ground. One of their favorite songs was playing in his car, and she demanded he pull over and turn it up. She dragged him out of the car, and the two of the danced and played in the rain. That was the day she knew she loved him. They were so young, but even then, she knew he was her forever.

It was getting late, and the rain was showing no sign of letting up. She spent most of the afternoon and beginning of the evening putting away supplies and getting ready for the following day. However, after she delivered dinner to Maria, she didn't have anything to distract her. During her trip to town, she had invested some of her money into some alcohol. She told herself it was partly so she could offer Damion some drinks with his dinner on the nights she did cook for him. However, she bought extra for herself.

It was officially five years to the day since Paul passed away. She hadn't slept at all in two days, and it was starting to take its toll on her. She needed sleep, and she was bound and determined to get some, even if she had to force herself to pass out.

Damion seemed to notice she was off. He hadn't poked fun at her as much as he usually would. They had a little banter over the biscuits but nothing else. The morning overall had been cold. At least he hadn't caught her crying.

Turning up the music she was playing, she started to sing along as she took shot after shot straight from the bottle of vodka in her hand. She wasn't sure how long she sat there, singing along and watching the rain pour down, but time had passed, and she grinned a bit seeing a soaking wet Damion and his girl of the night race over to his trailer. He turned to kiss her as he fumbled to get the door open. At least someone was going to have a good night.

Naomi wondered if he had ever had a woman stay the whole night with him. She had noticed that when he brought a girl to the trailer, he always sent her away a couple of hours later. It had to be a lonely life. She knew her life was lonely, but she had her reasons. If she were dating, she wasn't sure she would bring someone home that she wouldn't want to stay the whole night, but it wasn't her life.

Again, time seemed to lose meaning. She drank, she sang, and she drifted away to the sound of the rain. Tears rolled down her cheeks, and she didn't even try to stop them. The warmth of her tears thawed the ice of her pain.

CHAPTER ELEVEN

DAMION

J ulia had been a good distraction, but it was time for her to go. She
was getting dressed and doing the same thing all of his dates did.

"You sure you don't want me to stay? We could have a nice morning," she said looking over her shoulder as she snapped her bra together.

"No, I get up really early so I can prepare for work," he answered,
standing and fastening his pants. He pulled out a cigarette and lit it up
as he walked her to the door. "I had a good time."

"So did I. Call me?" she asked her final question of hope.

"Drive safe. This weather is hell," he answered, ignoring the question as he always did.

With the door open, she leaned up on tiptoes to give him a final kiss
before racing down the road to her car. It wasn't far, and he watched
her to make sure she made it. Almost out of habit, he looked across
the yard to Naomi's RV and was shocked to see her still sitting in her
chair out front. It was raining so hard that he couldn't hear her, but he
could swear he saw her lips moving. Checking his watch, he saw it was

after two in the morning, and he knew Naomi got up really early to start breakfast. Filming was probably going to be canceled again, but she didn't know that.

Curiosity got the better of him, so he braved the rain to walk across the yard to her. She was twirling a ring around her fingers. It was connected to a chain, and her actions came off more like a habit than anything else.

"It's pretty late," he said leaning on the awning post.

"Is it? I wouldn't know," she answered, holding her bare wrist up for him to see. "How was your date?"

"Fine," he answered, moving into her space more and taking a seat in the second chair. That was when he saw the empty bottles of vodka sitting at her feet. Another was in her hand, but she seemed to just be holding it more than anything else.

"Just fine?" she asked, giving him a wicked smile.

"Yeah, just fine," he answered.

"Well, that might be the saddest thing you have ever said to me. A date that ends like that should be more than fine," she said, catching him off guard.

"All my dates end like that," Damion said and shook his head, realizing how bad that actually made him sound.

"Still sad." Naomi laughed, leaning in closer to him. She was still wearing the jeans and white T-shirt, but she was dry again.

"How much have you had to drink?" he asked, feeling like he should check on her well-being a bit, even though she was teasing him.

"I don't know. How many bottles do you see?" she answered. She turned to look where she had been setting them, but lost her balance, and he reached over to steady her.

"Too many. Come on, let me get you to bed so you can sleep some of this off," he offered, standing and moving closer to her.

"I don't want to go to bed," she protested like a child.

"I know, but you need some sleep," he continued, helping her to her feet.

She wobbled forward and landed on his chest. For a moment the heat of her against him made a chill run down his spine. She took a little longer than he expected to steady herself, and her eyes closed for a moment.

She pushed off of him a bit and looked up at him. "I don't sleep," she said as if it was the sanest answer for her refusal. He knew she was restless. He had heard her screams and seen her up at all hours, but not sleeping at all was impossible. "Your chest is hard."

He laughed and helped steady her before stepping back again. "Why don't you sleep?" he asked before reaching to get another cigarette.

Naomi snatched it from his mouth with faster reflexes than he expected for someone that drunk. "I hate it when you smoke. It ruins you for me."

"Does it now? Okay, well let me get that from you then," he said, pointing to the bottle of vodka still in her hand.

She passed it over to him, and he took a drink from it. The liquid burned all the way down, and he realized she had gotten the cheap stuff. "Damn, you are trying to kill someone with this shit."

Naomi busted out laughing and then took the bottle back before taking another drink herself. The song changed, and she squealed in delight. Taking his hand, she started to pull him out into the rain. "I love this song! Dance with me!" she exclaimed.

He was already wet from walking over to her RV, but she had been relatively dry. That didn't last as he stumbled with her into the rain. He turned her and pulled her into him to help hold her up as he danced with her. He wasn't sure why he was giving in to her, but it was the first time he had really spent time with her, and she seemed to be having a great time. He stole the bottle of vodka from her again and took another drink, larger than the first. The heat of its effects started to spread through him, and he found himself laughing along with her.

They twirled and swayed as the song played on. He felt young and alive in a way no one else had made him feel in a long time. His life had been all about work and keeping people at a distance. Naomi wasn't allowing for any of that. She was pressed up to him as tightly as possible. He could feel her curves and muscles as she moved and swayed, and his heart started to pound hard and fast.

"You smell like jasmine and vodka," he whispered into her hair as the next song came on. It was slower, so he held her and slowly danced back and forth. It had to have been the single most intimate moment of his whole life, and fear was threatening to make him run.

"You smell like sex and smoke," she answered with a giggle.

"Sounds about right," he answered. He hadn't bothered to put on a shirt, so he was sure his night was heavy on his skin even with the rain.

They held each other close for several more moments before he realized that her body was shaking. He looked down in time to see her rub her cheek against his chest. Her face was wrinkled up and he knew she was crying. He started to ask her what had happened, but the song changed, and she started to dance faster again.

That was a mistake, though. She lost her footing and the two of them went tumbling down into the mud below them. Wet and dirty, they laughed hard. Damion's eyes ran up and down over Naomi's body, and he knew he needed to get away from her. This whole situation was asking for trouble.

"Come on. Let's go sit down. I think you are getting me drunk," he said, helping her back up.

They made their way back to the chairs, and she pulled him closer to her so he could continue to help keep her stable. "So, why don't you sleep?"

"I just don't," she answered, her face getting serious. He knew she wasn't getting sober, but something had changed. It was like his question brought out a soberness in her that was more powerful than the alcohol.

"That isn't an answer," Damion whispered, moving in closer. "I know we don't know each other well, but come on. You can tell me."

"Have you ever been in love?" Naomi asked, completely changing the subject.

The question threw him off, and he blinked a couple of times. "No, I haven't."

"That's now the saddest thing you have ever told me. All those girls and never in love. I don't think I could imagine a life like that," she said, taking another drink of the vodka.

Damion took the bottle from her and took his own drink before placing it out of her reach. "What about you? Have you ever been in love?"

"Yes, and it was the most magical thing in my life," she answered. Her voice sounded haunted, and her gaze became distant as if she was seeing something he couldn't.

"What happened?" he asked, not sure if he was ready for the answer.

Naomi was silent for so long that he thought she wasn't going to answer. "He died. Five years ago," she answered. He watched as tears began to stream down her cheeks. "He was my everything, and now he is just gone."

"I'm sorry to hear that," Damion whispered, reaching over and taking her hand.

"Not your fault. Sorry, I didn't mean to get like this. We were having so much fun," Naomi said, trying to pull herself together. She frantically wiped at her face trying to remove the evidence of her despair.

"It's fine," Damion answered, watching her.

"I thought I was going to be okay, but the closer it got the worse the nightmares got. I'm so tired," she said and started to look around. She was looking for the vodka, but he had it far enough away from her that she couldn't find it.

"You will be okay eventually. I'm sure it is harder than any other relationship since you loved him," he said, not sure what else to say.

"There never was any other relationship," Naomi confessed, and Damion found himself speechless.

"What do you mean? You've never been with anyone else?" he asked.

"Nope, just him. He was my one. My first kiss, my first, well, everything," she answered and smiled. Her cheeks turned slightly pink, which made him smile.

"Wow, now that is something. I don't think I could even give you a number for me. I lost count somewhere along the way and stopped bothering," he said, realizing just how much of a man whore he really was.

"Yeah well, you are zero still because you said you didn't love any of them," she said.

"So, you are at one and one, I'm at infinity and zero. That seems really off balanced."

"It is," she said giving him a serious look. Her hand reached up and moved his hair back from his face. The touch was soft and made him shiver, but she didn't even seem to realize what she was doing.

He watched her for a few seconds. Her eyes were heavy, and she was fighting sleep. Deciding she needed to go to bed regardless whether she wanted to, he picked her up and threw her over his shoulder.

"What are you doing?" she asked, wiggling as he opened the door to her RV and stepped inside. For a moment she was swatting at his ass, and he wasn't sure if he should be amused or offended.

"You need to go to bed. I'm helping you," he answered.

He made his way toward the back, and when he found the bed, he stood her next to it. He wasn't sure if he should just help her in soaking wet or wait for her to change. "I really don't want to go to bed."

"I know, but ummm, why don't you get some dry clothes on, and I will sit and talk with you until you fall asleep. Deal?" he suggested.

"Alright," she answered and then pulled off her shirt.

He turned so fast he almost hit the wall. He was a bit too big for her place.

After a few minutes he heard the rustling of her blankets, and he turned to see her crawling into the bed. He sat down next to her and smiled. "Alright, well, if it helps, you don't have to make me breakfast. I'll have leftovers."

"I'll be fine. I'll have breakfast for you just as usual," she said.

It didn't take her long to fall asleep. He knew it was the alcohol pulling her under, but at least she was going to get some sleep. He started to leave, but her hand flung out and grabbed his wrist as she sat straight up screaming. The look of pure fear on her face was startling. She stared out into the darkness like she had just escaped hell.

He squeezed her hand, and she slowly turned to look at him. "I'm sorry."

CHAPTER TWELVE

DAMION

He had finally left Naomi's RV as the sun was rising. She hadn't been able to get to sleep but had managed to sober up. The rain was still pouring down, and the stretch of land between her RV and his trailer was almost a swamp, splashing mud up on his pants. He needed a cigarette, a shower, and three days of sleep, in that order.

Naomi had gotten up and gone to start the day's meals. Even though he told her not to bother, she insisted, and he started to realize that staying busy kept her from thinking too much. He couldn't help but wonder what more there was to this story. She had told him about her ex dying, but why did she wake up in such panic? Why didn't she sleep? Only one person could answer that question, or at least he hoped she could.

Lighting a cigarette, he sat down on his bed and dialed Jessie's number. It was early, but he hoped she was awake. She answered on the second ring. "Damion? What's wrong?"

"Nice to talk to you, too," he answered, blowing out the smoke. He could feel the calming effects rushing through his veins, yet part of him wanted to toss it away. "Nothing's wrong. How are you?"

"Damion, you don't call someone at sunrise just to chat. What's wrong?" Jessie insisted. He could hear her shifting around and got the feeling she was still in bed.

"I wanted to ask you something about Naomi. I feel like you might be the only one who can answer it," he said, feeling a bit guilty for going behind Naomi's back.

"Pretty sure she can answer questions herself, but sure. I'm waiting for the coffee to be ready. What do you want to know?" Jessie groaned.

"Why doesn't she sleep?" he asked, coming right out with it.

"Ah," she said, and there was a long moment of silence. "Has she told you about Paul?"

"Maybe, she told me about her ex who died," he answered.

"Yeah, that's Paul. What did she tell you?" Jessie asked. Usually she was sarcastic and silly, but her voice was so serious he worried he had stumbled into something deeper than he was prepared for. "I really shouldn't be talking to you about this."

"Please, something happened last night, and I need to know," he nearly begged. He found himself pacing his trailer, his heart pounding in time with his steps.

"What do you mean something happened?" Jessie asked, concern in her voice. "Do I need to come out there?"

"No, everything is fine. We are just. We spent time together, and I finally got her to go to bed, and she was asleep like fifteen minutes before she woke up screaming and never went back to sleep. I hear her all the time waking up screaming like that, but seeing her do it... It was chilling. Now what happened?" he demanded, hating the runaround.

"Okay, but if she gets mad at me, I'm going to come kick your ass, and you can't fight back because you can't hit a pregnant woman," Jessie said. "So, she told you Paul died, but I imagine she didn't tell you how. Well, he had been in a car accident."

"That doesn't make sense why she would be so upset," Damion interrupted. Car accidents happened all the time.

"Do you want me to tell you or not?" Jessie yelled, and he shut up instantly. "It wasn't a bad accident. He had some scrapes and bruises. The car was totaled, but all in all, nothing bad happened. So, after a quick look-over, the hospital sent him home. Well, as you can imagine, he was tired, so they went to bed early. No big deal, right?"

"Yeah," Damion whispered, lighting another cigarette. The tone in Jessie's voice said so much more than her words.

"Well, when she woke up, she was cold. Like really cold. She tried to move, but he was holding her really tightly. She tried to wake him up so she could get up, but he wouldn't wake up. She was cold because he was dead. He had died holding her in their sleep. She woke up to a dead body wrapped around her," Jessie explained.

Damion was sure he didn't breathe for several minutes as the thought of that sank in. The horror that had to have been. He was pretty sure he wouldn't sleep anymore after that either. Not knowing what to say, he let Jessie continue.

"She started screaming so loud that we could hear her from across the street. Brad and I threw on our robes and ran across the street. Brad managed to get her pried out, and we pulled her out of the room, but it took drugs to get her to calm down. Autopsy said he had died from a blood clot going to his brain. It killed him instantly, and he supposedly didn't feel it. Apparently, he had some sort of blood disease that made his blood clot really easily. It isn't something they test for really, so no one knew. He literally died because of a minor injury in a car accident, and no one knew it would happen. Naomi was devastated. She sold everything, closed her business, everything. They were about to get married. I thought I was going to lose her too. I would sleep over with her or have her stay with me and hold her, but I'm married. I had to live my life."

Silence grew between them as Damion processed what his friend had just told him. No wonder she didn't want to sleep. The idea of waking up to the one you love dead would make anyone sleepless. His heart hurt, and all he could think of was trying to find a way to help her. It didn't matter that it wasn't his place. He wanted to do something.

"I couldn't imagine," he finally said.

"Yeah, me either, and I was there. She hasn't been the same since. It's why I recommended her to work for you. I was hoping getting away would help, but last night was five years. I was surprised she didn't call me, but I was hoping she was so busy with you and such that it wasn't bothering her too much," Jessie admitted.

"Well, she was drunk. We hung out when I got back from my date," he answered. "Thanks for sharing that with me."

"Yeah, just, watch out for her. I worry about her," Jessie said in a very motherly voice.

"You are going to be a great mom," he said, and after a few more pleasantries, he got off the phone.

While he showered, his mind raced. Helping Naomi seemed like his new purpose. There had to be a reason they had been brought together, that he had been the one to see her last night when everyone else was asleep. What would have happened if he hadn't gone to check on her? That was a question he didn't want the answer to.

No longer tired, he got dressed and went in search of Maria. The weather was still horrible, but he needed some things from town. A plan was forming in his mind, and stupid as it might be, he couldn't think of a better one.

"Hey, you know they canceled the shoot for today. Right?" Maria said when he walked into her trailer.

"Yeah, but I need you to do me a favor," he said pulling a list out of his pocket. "Can you get this stuff for me?"

Maria studied the list and then looked up at him with one eyebrow arched. "Nicotine patches? You planning to quit smoking?"

"No, but I'm thinking I might cut back," he answered. It was half true. He needed them for if Naomi spent the night with him. If she was in his trailer, he didn't want to smell like smoke. "Oh, and I need my trailer cleaned and my bedding washed fresh. I want to get rid of the smoke smell. From now on, I am going to smoke outside."

"Damion, what's going on?" Maria asked, setting the list down on her desk.

"You are going to think it's stupid, and I honestly don't want to hear you reprimand me right now," he answered, sitting back and leaning his head against the wall.

"Now I need to know," Maria insisted, smacking him on the leg. "What are you up to?"

"It's complicated, but Naomi, well she has a lot of trouble sleeping, so I was thinking she could stay with me, and I could help her sleep," he answered, knowing his words sounded ridiculous.

"Fucking your employees is the worst idea. There is a reason you date randos all the time."

"No! I'm not talking about fucking her. I mean it, just sleeping. I sleep on my side of the bed; she sleeps on hers. Clothes on, pillow between, I have it all figured out," Damion responded. Damn he sounded like an idiot.

"That isn't any better. Damion, you have never shared a bed with anyone. Even when you consistently dated Allicia, you didn't sleep in the same bed with her. You do realize this is going to put you in a very compromising position. You are asking for lawsuits and a ruined career. I will not support this lunacy," Maria said, pushing the list back toward him.

"No, I'm not. I swear. This is all platonic. You don't understand. She needs it, and I don't know. I feel like I need it too. Please, just go get this stuff and help me get the trailer cleaned. I do believe I'm the one who pays you." Damion knew he came off sounding like a jerk, but he didn't care. Arguing with her was not part of the plan.

"Yes, you pay me to keep your ass out of trouble, and this is nothing but trouble," Maria huffed but got up and reached for her purse. "I want it on the record that I told you this is a really stupid idea. Okay."

"Noted," he answered and watched her walk out.

CHAPTER THIRTEEN

NAOMI

Everything felt bad. Her body ached. Her head ached. Everything sucked. When she went to clean up her mess, she realized she had drunk enough vodka to be hospitalized and wasn't sure how she was still standing. Damion had told her not to bother with cooking, but she needed to. It kept her mind busy. The distraction was everything to her.

She had just finished lunch when she heard the door open. Damion walked in, wet and sexy, and part of her brain from the night before remembered dancing with him in the rain. Paul used to dance with her in the rain. It had been special, and part of her felt like she betrayed him by dancing with Damion like that. Yet she felt like she needed it.

"Hey, Naomi, you in here?" he asked, coming to the kitchen door.

"Yeah, back here. I'll be right out with your food," she answered, picking up the plate.

"Bring you some too. I want to talk," he said.

She hadn't even made herself a plate, so she had to take a moment to throw something together for herself. Not that she wanted to eat. Her stomach contracted at the thought of food.

"Sorry I'm running a bit late. Long night and all," she said, placing his food in front of him before sitting next to him.

"Yeah, I was there. Remember?" he said with a devilish smile.

Had she done something even more stupid than she could remember? She had been so drunk that the memories were blurry.

"Yeah, you were. I'm so sorry. That was very unprofessional of me. I swear, I used my own money for the alcohol, and that will never happen again. It's just, well, yesterday was just a bad day," she tried to explain without going into details about Paul. The last thing she needed was to break down crying on him... again. Out of habit she began to play with the ring she wore.

"Yeah, I know. Jessie told me about Paul," Damion said, his face turning serious.

Naomi's breath caught and her eyes grew wide. Jessie shouldn't have told him about any of that.

"And before you get mad at her, I made her tell me. I needed to know what was going on. You were a mess last night."

"It's..." she started to say, but he reached out and placed his hand on hers. His face grew soft, and she got the feeling he actually cared. It was odd because most of the time he seemed pretty indifferent to her.

"I wanted to talk to you about your inability to sleep. It's not a good thing, and getting drunk obviously doesn't help either. So, I have an idea. A crazy idea," he said as he started working on his lunch.

Naomi watched him for a moment, her own plate there more for decoration than anything else. "What's your idea?"

"I want you to sleep with me," he said as if he was telling her about the weather.

"Ummm, I don't think that will help," she said, heat flooding her face.

"No, damn, I got distracted by how good the food is. I want you to sleep in my bed with me. Fully clothed and with pillows between us. You come over, we hang out, and then we go to sleep. Jessie said she used to do that with you, and it helped," Damion explained.

That allowed her to calm down. Sure, she had thought about having sex with Damion before, but as a fangirl teenager, not in reality.

"You're right. That is crazy," she answered. "Besides, you will smell like smoke and I'm sure your trailer does as well. I don't think I could sleep like that, and you are too tall for my bed."

She was coming up with excuses, and she knew it. If her life had been different, she would have jumped at the chance to get into Damion Malcom's bed, but things weren't different.

"I'm taking care of all of that. My whole trailer is being cleaned as we speak, Maria went to get me some of those patches, and I will make sure to shower and brush my teeth before getting in bed. No smoke smell," he said, his smile turning soft, almost sweet.

"Why do you want to do this?" she asked softly. He had really put thought into this insane plan of his.

"I don't know. I want to help, and if this will help, I want to do it," he answered. "I swear, nothing more than friends helping each other."

"We aren't really much of friends," she said, laughing a bit.

"Last night changed that. Come on, try it one night. If it's a disaster, we will know and can just go back to normal," he said as if that was the end of it.

Her head hurt too much for her to argue, and honestly, the idea of not being alone did seem nice. "Okay, but as friends, clothes on, pillow between us," she reiterated.

"Yep, friends." He smiled and held his hand out to shake hers. "See you tonight."

She had no idea what to expect. All day her heart had been racing with what to expect. Damion had told her to come over after eight. With the bad weather, no one had done anything. He hadn't even gone out on a date like usual. With a small bag of stuff, Naomi walked across the little road to Damion's trailer. She couldn't help but think this was a stupid idea, but she had agreed to do it.

She knocked on the door, and Damion swung it open. He was running a towel through his hair to dry it after his shower, but he already had pajama bottoms on. They looked new, and she wondered if he didn't usually sleep with clothes on. "Am I early?"

"No, I'm just running a couple of minutes late. Come on in," he answered, moving out of the way. He closed and locked the door. "Make yourself at home. I didn't know if you preferred a certain side of the bed, so it's your choice. I already set up the pillow wall."

Naomi smiled, seeing all the effort he had put into this. If nothing else, he was trying to help, and she couldn't begrudge him that. "I'll sleep on the far side if that's alright."

"Perfect. Um, can you help me with this?" he asked, holding out one of the nicotine patches. He was really being serious about all of this, and it made her heart ache just a bit.

"Yeah, I can. I feel bad putting you out," she said, opening the patch and putting it on his arm as the instructions suggested. It had been a long time since she had done anything close to this, and helping him get ready for bed, as innocent as it might seem, was more intimate than she had realized it would be.

"You aren't. I'm the one who came up with this plan. I just also know I'm not used to a whole night without a cigarette. I'll live, though," he answered and then found his shirt and tossed it on. "You want to watch a movie or something? I figure eight is a little too early to go to bed, but I wanted you to feel comfortable and acclimated before trying to sleep."

"Yeah, we can do that," she answered. "I'm going to go get changed into my pajamas first."

"Help yourself. I got an extra toothbrush in there for you and some girl stuff. Well, Okay, I had Maria get stuff. I wasn't sure if you would need anything," he answered, showing her to the bathroom.

It was nice, all the effort he had gone to for this. She had a feeling it was a waste, but it was sweet of him to try. Once she was changed, she went out to the bedroom. Damion was already under the covers and had pulled the covers down on her side. She slowly made her way around the bed and sat down before pulling her hair up to put on her bonnet.

"What is that?" he asked, a hint of laughter in his voice.

"It's a bonnet. It's good for your hair. I almost always sleep with one. Honestly you should too. It protects your hair. I bet your hairdresser would notice a difference," she answered, tying it up and grinning at him. She knew she looked a bit silly, but she hoped it also made her look less enticing. Not that she thought she was his type.

"I'll pass, but you look cute," he said, clicking on the TV. She got comfortable, sitting back against the pillows and headboard so she could watch the movie. "What's your favorite movie?" he asked, pulling up a streaming service.

"You don't want to know the answer to that," she said and could feel the blush rising on her cheeks.

"Why wouldn't I want to know?" he asked, his face screwed up in confusion.

"Well, I didn't want to say anything, because I didn't want it to affect my job, but you are kinda my favorite actor," she answered. Her hands flung over her face to hide her embarrassment.

Damion laughed, and it only made her blush harder. "Okay, well, that doesn't answer my question. What is your favorite movie?"

"Redemption," she answered matter-of-factly.

"Alright, well, *Redemption* it is," he said and went about pulling it up.

"No, I'm sure you don't want to watch one of your old movies." She leaned over and tried to take the remote. He tossed it to his other hand and continued, pushing her back in a playful manner.

"I don't care what we watch. I just want to do something that makes you happy and more relaxed. Besides, I haven't seen that since the premiere. It will be like my first time," he answered.

They were both laughing, and it felt nice to just laugh. For a moment there was no stress or tension. It was just the two of them being friends. Then the movie started, and she turned her focus to it. Naomi didn't realize when he dimmed the lights. She didn't see him watching her more than the movie. Her focus was on the movie, and how it always made her feel. At one point, she started to cry, and he handed her a tissue without saying a word.

The movie was full of love, hope, despair, heartache, and everything in between. It had always been her favorite movie—the one she could watch no matter what, and it would take her away from the real world. Her copy of it had been destroyed by how many times she watched it, and she had been thankful when streaming became a thing.

When the movie was over, she blinked and looked around as if she had just been pulled out of a different world. He wasn't watching the movie. Damion was watching her, and it made her feel exposed and vulnerable. She found herself pulling the blanket up over her as if to cover up her nakedness, even though she was fully dressed.

"I didn't mean to make you cry," he whispered and handed her another tissue.

"You didn't. That movie is just so good. How do you do it?" she asked, for the first time being able to ask the questions she had always wondered about.

"How do I do what?" he asked.

"Make it look like you are really in love," she added, hoping it would make her question make more sense.

"I don't know. I just pretend like I am in love, and it seems to work," he answered. Naomi wasn't sure she would ever be able to do that. "You ready to get some sleep? I'm still exhausted after staying up all night."

"Umm," she had no idea how to answer that. No, she didn't want to sleep. She never wanted to sleep. "I guess."

"Hey, I'm right here, okay. If you need me, I'm right here," he answered and squeezed her hand.

She snuggled down into the bed and did her best to get comfortable. Damion turned off the light, and they were lulled into calm by the sound of the rain outside. She rolled, facing their little pillow wall and placed her hand on it. Damion was looking at her and he reached over and squeezed her hand again. He was certainly going above and beyond.

Chapter Fourteen

Damion

He watched her as she started to fall asleep. His hand stayed steady on hers, and he softly rubbed his thumb against her in a comforting way. This was the first time he ever had anyone spend the night in his bed, and his head was racing. It wasn't how he thought it would be, but strangely it felt right. After she had been asleep for a few minutes, he found himself following her into the darkness, the weight of a long night and day taking its toll.

Somewhere in the time they were asleep, Naomi had tossed the pillow wall out of the way. He had awakened only for a moment when she took his hand and pulled him to her. Part of him wanted to pull away, knowing it was a bad idea, but he was too tired to fight it. So he moved in closer, wrapped his arm around her, buried his face against her jasmine scented skin, and went back to sleep. It was the most comfortable sleep he had ever gotten, and it only lasted about ten more minutes before she pushed up, screaming into the darkness and swatting away at her shoulders and arms.

He sat up next to her and moved in closer to pull her to him. "Hey, Naomi, I'm here. You're okay. I'm here," he whispered to her, trying to pull her out of the horror of her thoughts.

Her eyes were still distant when she turned to look at him. She was terrified, and she started to cry. He reached up and cupped her cheek. His other hand stroked her hair, making the bonnet fall away. Damn, she was beautiful, even in that state.

"I'm sorry," she whispered.

"It's okay. I'm here. That's what this was all for," he answered. He kept petting her and held her gaze until her eyes softened and he knew that whatever she was seeing had left and she was back from her nightmare. "Let's try to lie back down okay."

"What happened to the pillow wall?" she asked, looking around.

"You threw it on the floor. I can put it back, though," he said, moving to reach for it.

Naomi stopped him, and he turned to look at her. "No, that's okay. I mean, if you don't mind."

"I don't mind," he answered. He lay back down and held his arms out.

Hesitantly Naomi joined him and pressed her cheek against his chest. "How long was I asleep?"

"About an hour. Come on. Let's go for two now," he said. He found himself petting her hair again and watched as she drifted back to sleep. It took him significantly longer to fall back to sleep, but eventually he joined her.

The sun was rising when his eyes cracked open. Naomi was still lying against his chest. There was a little wet spot where he assumed she had either cried or drooled, neither of which bothered him. She was still asleep, which meant their experiment had been a success. Of course, they had already broken one of the rules, but if it helped her sleep, he didn't care.

Naomi started to shift and move before lifting her head. She looked around the room, and he could tell she felt a little lost. Then she jumped and pushed away, a look of shock coming across her face. "What time is it?"

Damion hadn't even checked yet, so he looked at his watch. "Just after six. I need to get up and work out."

"What? That means I," she stuttered, looking around. She started searching around the bed trying to find something.

"You slept all night. How do you feel?" he asked, moving back to his side of the bed and getting up.

"Honestly, I don't know yet. I feel late, and unsure. And where is my bonnet?" she answered, throwing the blanket around.

Damion went to her side of the bed and picked it up off the floor. "It came off and I didn't bother to fix it. You seemed not to care so much."

Naomi snatched the bonnet from him and then got up. He couldn't tell if something was wrong, or if she just didn't know what to think of everything. Either way, her reaction was making him laugh.

"Are you laughing at me?"

"Nope, I'm laughing at the situation. I'll leave you to get dressed. I'm going for my run. I'll see you at breakfast?" he said, heading toward the bathroom. He had put his workout clothes in there so he could change if she was still here.

"Oh shit! I'm late getting breakfast started. I'm sorry!" she called from the other side of the door. He could hear her fight with the door to leave then slam it behind her when she did.

With her gone, he was able to process what had happened. He had spent the night with a woman—a beautiful, sweet, caring woman who needed him. They hadn't kissed. They hadn't flirted. It had been so innocent, yet he couldn't get the smell of her skin out of his head. His mind swirled with the thought of her, and it was anything but friendship. A feeling he had never had tugged at him, and he could hear Maria in his mind telling him how stupid he had been.

Strangely, he had no desire to change his actions. If she wanted, he would have her stay with him every night. He was sure he could keep it platonic, regardless of how much he would love to see what happened next. This was about helping Naomi, not him.

Pushing his thoughts away, he went for his run. When he got back, he had his first cigarette in over twelve hours. Strangely, it was not nearly as satisfying as he thought it would be, and after two puffs he put it out and threw it away.

CHAPTER FIFTEEN

NAOMI

She was still shaking as she plated Damion's breakfast. What had they been thinking? Nothing they had said stayed. The wall was gone, and she snuggled to his body as if they had been sleeping together for years. He had gone out of his way to make her comfortable, but she knew it wasn't a good idea to keep it up. If they did, she wasn't sure she would be able to keep her emotions in check. It had been a long time since she had a man in her life, and loneliness was a powerful emotion. Paul deserved better from her than that. She owed him the decency of not just falling into bed with the first man to offer.

Yet in a way she had.

They hadn't done anything untoward. Snuggling wasn't a sin. She and Jessie often snuggled as friends, so what made it different with Damion? Probably the fact that part of her wanted to know what it was like to play with his hair and kiss his lips. School girl crush aside, the real Damion was right in front of her and being a better friend than she could have ever expected.

Shaking off her thoughts, she gathered the plates and went out to the dining table. Damion was towel drying his hair still and smiled when he saw her come through the door. She couldn't help but smile back at him when she saw him. Setting the plates down on the table, she went over the meal as she did every morning.

"So, I made you a ham, cheese, and vegetable omelet with a side of cantaloupe and biscuits," she said.

Her brow arched toward him in challenge as she placed the biscuits, nice and fresh from the oven, right in front of him. They had been fighting with this little banter from the start, and she looked forward to it every day. She was wasting a lot of flour and ingredients on it, but she refused to back down.

"When are you going to give it up, Naomi. I'm not eating your biscuits," he said, pushing them away. The plate slid until it was over the halfway point of the table. However, he gave her a sly, challenging smile.

"Really, you spent all night with me and can't even take one bite of my biscuits?" she said, a more seductive tone in her voice than she had intended. Of course, she had to play it up and leaned in very close to him where he could easily get a view down her tank top.

He looked, which made her smile. Cheap shot or not, this was war. "Well, if you are going to throw it in my face, you are going to have to do a hell of a lot more than sleep on my chest to make me eat biscuits."

"Really? I don't think so. You will give in one day," Naomi answered. She took a seat in the chair closest to him and took one of the biscuits off of the plate. Tearing a small piece off of it, she waved it right in front of his mouth before popping it into her own mouth and moaning in delight. "You'll get tired of missing out on the true pleasures of life one day and give in to your baser instincts."

Damion leaned in close to her and whispered his next response in her ear. The feel of his warm breath on her skin sent shivers down her spine. "You can play dirty all you want. You aren't winning this one. Now, I need to eat and get to set."

She couldn't help bursting out in laughter to break the sexual tension that had built between them. Getting up from the table, she went back into the kitchen to work on the rest of the day's meal plans. However, as she passed by the door, she did catch him picking up the biscuit and investigating it. He didn't try it, but he thought about it, and that was a small victory.

Getting caught up in her work, she couldn't help but appreciate feeling more awake. She couldn't remember the last time she had gotten a whole night's sleep. For the first time in years, she didn't feel like her head was foggy, and her body didn't ache. In all honesty, she probably could have slept the rest of the day and not noticed.

It was odd that Damion's insane plan had actually worked. However, there was no way there would be a repeat. He had his own life, which didn't include her. How was he supposed to entertain his "dates" if she was hanging around all the time? No, she appreciated his help, but she knew it wasn't a solution, just an experiment.

With lunch finished and dinner slow-roasting, Naomi got busy cleaning out the fridge and cupboard, making sure nothing was expired or running low. She used that time to build a shopping list and a menu for the upcoming week. Even though she had just gone to town, she liked to stay on top of things. That way when she made her next trip, she would be less likely to forget anything.

The weather was nicer than it had been in days, and since she was finished in the kitchen, she decided to take a walk. They were in a national forest, and nature was always calming. Her mind wandered to various things. When she was younger, Paul would take her hiking and swimming. It had been some of her favorite dates since it was much more difficult to get caught up in the busy world around them. No phones, no internet, just the two of them enjoying time together. Jessie had tried to invite her to go camping with her and Brad, but Naomi felt like she would have been the third wheel, which was the last thing she wanted.

Being out in the woods now made her feel alive again. It felt like Paul was there, guiding her. Maybe he wanted her to heal. Maybe he had put all of this into motion like some sort of guardian angel. It certainly made it more important for her not just to become some sort of floozy, jumping at another man. Did people even use the word floozy anymore? Either way, she was going to enjoy the happy moments while she could and see this as a healing process.

Chapter Sixteen

Damion

His mouth moved over hers in a fluid motion. His hand gripped her ass and lifted her up before turning her to slam her against the wall. They made out with heat and passion, and he fed from those lips like they held the elixir of life. Her hands gripped into his hair, and he moaned deeply, wanting more. He pressed tighter to her and broke the kiss to trail his lips down her neck. His mind was lost, his world was spinning.

"*Cut!*" the director screamed, breaking the trance Damion had found himself in. "Damion, love the enthusiasm, but you are moving too fast, and your head was blocking the camera. We will need to do this again. This time, you have to move the other way."

"Damn, what got into you?" Allicia said, her breath heavy.

He wasn't about to answer that, partly because he didn't want to admit it to himself. Whatever was going on, his relationship with Naomi was professional and platonic. There was no pushing further. At least not while she worked for him. No, there would never be a way for them to be together. She was sweet and innocent, and he was a globetrotting man whore. She deserved better, and the last thing he needed was a relationship distracting him from work.

"Nothing, just, feeling the scene today," he answered, smiling at his costar. It didn't stop his mind from conjuring up all kinds of fantasies, especially after a night of holding her.

"I can tell. I still think the two of us should make more of this. We are so good together," she said, moving in closer to him. Her fingers played along the skin of his temple and pushed his hair back a bit.

Allicia was gorgeous, the type of beauty that stopped men in their tracks when she walked by, but he knew it was all a mask. She was just as focused on her career as he was. The only reason she wanted to pursue something with him was because she knew it would boost them on social media and promote the movie.

"Alli, we are not good together, and you know that. We tried, and neither of us want a real relationship. We work well together, so let's stick with that," he answered and kissed her forehead.

She wasn't having it and pushed him back. "You have never kissed me like you just did. Don't tell me that was just about work!"

Damion stood there as Allicia stormed off, tossing a random water bottle she came across on her way. Her temper was getting the better of her, and she was proving just how much of a diva she really was. Everyone in the room looked back and forth between the two of them, and he had no idea what to say.

Maria came up to him and handed him a bottle of water. "Do I even want to know?"

"Probably not," he answered, opening the bottle and taking a drink.

"Did something happen last night?" she asked and stared at him with a stern look in her eyes.

"No, nothing happened. We slept and that's it," he answered, keeping his voice low.

Some people on sets were always looking for information to sell. It was far too easy to get in trouble by saying too much in the presence of others.

"Yeah, tell that to your costar there. Look, I still think this was a bad idea, and I hope you got it out of your system. Don't fuck this up for us. I depend on you doing well," she said. He knew she cared about him and didn't want things going wrong, but she also depended on him for her livelihood. They had been in this together for a long time, and he had no intention of screwing her over.

"I'm not going to fuck anything up. Now, let me get back to work," he answered as he took another drink of water and handed the bottle back to her.

Allicia was back after a couple of minutes of throwing her fit, and filming got started again. Damion did his best to handle things how the director asked him, but he was having trouble concentrating. He wanted a different pair of lips on his. He wanted to fill his head with the scent of jasmine flowers and trace his fingers along a different jaw line, but this was work, and he did his job. The fight forgotten, Allicia did her job as well, and they got through the rest of the shoot without incident.

"Hey, so I know this little Mexican place just in town that is really good and has dancing. Do you want to go?" one of the girls working with catering asked. Damion had a reputation with taking girls out and usually appreciated a girl with the balls to ask him herself, but he wasn't in the mood to go out.

"I appreciate that, maybe another night. I have plans already," he answered. It was a lie. His only plans were to take a very cold shower, but he didn't want the girl to think he was just blowing her off after she got the courage to ask.

"I would like that. I'm here most days, so just let me know," she answered and handed over a card with her name and number on it.

"You aren't going out tonight?" Maria asked as he gathered up his things.

"No, not tonight. Why?" he asked. Usually, Maria didn't care what he did when he got off work.

"Honestly, I have gotten used to eating your dinner," she answered and laughed. "That girl can cook. Have you tried those biscuits she makes? Damn, I can't believe they are actually healthy."

Had Naomi put Maria up to saying that about her biscuits? It was their own private war that he couldn't wait to battle every day. In all honesty, he had gotten to the point he wanted to try them, but it was down to the principle of it all at that point. If he gave in, Naomi won, and he wasn't about to let that happen.

"No, I haven't. You know I don't eat carbs," Damion answered.

He and Maria walked back toward their trailers. "Well, you should. They are amazing. You would like them if you weren't such a stick in the mud."

"I'll take your word for it. Come on. I'll still share dinner with you," he said, and they continued walking. "You know, I don't think I have actually tried one of Naomi's dinners either. Not since we did the interview. I usually go out."

"I know! Which has been an advantage to me this whole time. Are you sure there isn't some girl you can run off with and get dinner? Give in to the carbs or something?" Maria teased.

"Well, I did get the number of a girl with catering. Should I give her a call? I'm sure she would be happy if I changed my plans," Damion said, holding out the card.

"Yes, call her, and leave me to my free meal," Maria said laughing. "Off with you!"

Damion burst out laughing too and didn't realize he almost ran into Naomi. She was standing there with a couple of to-go boxes in her hands and a shocked look. "What's going on?"

"Damion won't go out so I can have his dinner," Maria answered before he could say anything.

"Oh, well, it does seem to be his normal routine. I was actually going to meet up with you at your trailer," Naomi answered. "Are you actually staying for dinner tonight?"

For several seconds the silence created tension between all of them. Her eyes were hard to read, and it made him wonder what she was thinking. "Yeah, I didn't feel like going out tonight."

"Oh, well, good thing I always make enough for you too, just in case," Naomi answered and held a box out to Maria. "Your dinner, madam."

"I like this one, Damion. Don't fuck it up," Maria said, taking the box and turning to go to her own trailer.

"Is there something I need to know?" Naomi asked, walking back toward the kitchen trailer.

"No, she is just in a weird mood. How was your day?" he asked, not wanting to go into Maria's concerns. He had been all too happy for his agent to get distracted with the discussion of dinner.

"It was good. I went for a walk and enjoyed the sun a bit. What about you? Shoot go well?" she asked.

Damion opened the door, and Naomi entered. "Yeah, it was pretty good. Alli got pissed off at me for a bit, but that happens at least once a week."

"Why is that?" Naomi asked, setting the box down on the table before heading to the kitchen door.

"She wants to get back together, and I don't. Now and then she pushes, and I push back. She doesn't like hearing no," Damion explained, leaning against the door frame as he watched Naomi move around the kitchen.

She was an expert in every sense of the word. Her plating was always beautiful, and each item was measured out to ensure it fit into his diet. He loved her attention to detail, even in the midst of their very casual conversation.

"Didn't the two of you date before?" she asked, not looking up from the plate.

"Yeah, for a little while, but it never went anywhere. She wanted something I didn't want to give her," he answered.

Naomi grabbed the plate and headed toward him. He pushed away from the door and held it open for her as she went through. She set the plate down where he usually sat and reached to slide the to-go box toward her. "What's that?" she asked, continuing on with the conversation.

"Commitment," he answered. "I don't want that in my life. I don't even let girls spend the night with me. Not even Alli spent the night with me the whole time we were together."

"Wait, what? Like, you love 'em and then kick them out?" Naomi asked, sounding offended on behalf of all women.

"I'm not quite that big of a dick. I do the whole snuggle thing for a while, but no, I don't let them stay. I don't want anyone to stay," he answered.

"You let me stay. Why is that different?" she asked, and he could see the realization cross her face.

"We didn't do anything. I'm trying to help you. It has nothing to do with sex or relationships," he answered, hoping she didn't pick up on any of his bullshit.

"So you are a man whore and an asshole. Got it. You know, it wouldn't hurt to let a girl stay with you. It isn't like they are going to slip a wedding band on your finger and hex you into being their husband. Maybe you wouldn't be so lonely," she said.

"I don't know, Alli might," he answered, and the two of them laughed. "I think I will just continue to be an asshole man whore and not have to worry about it. Alli is the only one who has ever pushed for more. Most girls know what they are getting into."

"I see. I bet none of them actually think you will go through with it. Every single one of them probably thought they would be the one to change that," Naomi said before taking a bite of her meal.

He had never thought of it that way. The problem was, Naomi was the only girl he had ever met that he thought about changing it all for. Heat started to rise up in him again, and he did his best to shake it away. "Do you want to come over again tonight?"

Naomi looked at him shocked. "Again?"

"Yeah, I mean, don't you want to get good sleep again?" he asked, his words telling a lie his head wasn't ready to speak out loud. In his mind he was asking if she would let him hold her again.

"I'm not sure that's a good idea. Damion, this could easily get out of hand. I'm your employee and friend. We shouldn't confuse that," she answered, getting up. She picked up her box of food and started for the door.

He wanted to call out to her, but he stopped himself. No, she was right. If they spent every night together there was too much risk. Now he needed that cold shower.

CHAPTER SEVENTEEN

NAOMI

She was lying in bed, trying to see if she could sleep on her own. Would she be able to now that she had made progress with Damion? After a very cold shower, she had decided to put on her pajamas and lie down to give it a try. Her heart was pounding, and everything in her was fighting it. She didn't even have the benefit of being sleepy since she had gotten such a good night's sleep the night before. No way was Damion going to ruin her to where that was the only way she could sleep.

Pulling out her Kindle, she started reading a book to try and get her mind off of things. There were a couple of romance novels she had been meaning to read, and it was a good time to get started. Reading often relaxed her, and maybe it would help lull her to sleep. After a few chapters, her eyes got heavy, and she started to feel herself drift off. She let the feeling take her, and without realizing it, she fell asleep.

The sweetness of the book gave way to visions of Paul. They were at a park together, sitting on a large rock after hiking. The sun was setting, and they were enjoying some trail mix before getting ready to head back down the hill. It had been a perfect day.

"Naomi, I love you so much," he said, leaning over and kissing her. She moaned softly, feeling his lips on hers. She missed his kiss so much.

"I love you too. Why can't every day be like this day?" she asked, leaning her forehead against his.

"You know why," he whispered. "You are stronger than this, baby."

"No, I'm not," she answered, reaching up and gripping his shirt to pull him tighter to her. She didn't want to let go.

Paul wrapped his arms around her and held her tightly as the sun finished setting. Then the darkness spread over them, and the world got cold. Naomi tried to move, but she couldn't. She was stuck in the circle of Paul's frozen arms, and nothing she did broke her free.

"Let me go! Stop! No!" she screamed.

She fell out of the bed, kicking and pushing in the darkness to try and escape. Paul was gone. The park, the rock, everything was gone, and she was back in her RV. Cold sweat dripped down her face, and she needed to escape. With her heart racing, she stormed out of her RV and across the road to Damion's trailer. He answered almost instantly, and she pushed in past him, her mind still in the dream.

"Why? Why can't it be different?"

"Naomi, what happened?" Damion asked, shutting the door.

"My life wasn't supposed to be like this. Nothing was supposed to be like this!" she said, falling down onto the bed and burying her face in her hands. "Why is he gone?"

Damion didn't say anything. He just sat down next to her and pulled her into him. He smelled fresh, like sandalwood, without a hint of smoke on him. That surprised her, but she didn't have it in her to ask. Instead, she leaned against him and cried. This was so unprofessional, and she really shouldn't have been coming to him with her personal problems. This was throwing a wrench in his life, and he deserved better.

"I'm sorry. I shouldn't be here," she said, and started to get up, her hands wiping at her tear-soaked face.

"No, it's fine. You can stay," Damion said, reaching out and taking her hand to pull her back to the bed. "Stay and get some rest."

"This isn't fair to you," she said, looking down at him.

"It's my idea," he said and gave her a smile. "Come on. You know that I won't do anything, and you are safe here. So stay and get some rest. Do you want the pillow wall?"

He reached for the extra pillow and set it in the center of the bed where it had been the night before. Naomi didn't know what to say. Honestly, no she didn't want the pillow. She didn't want to be alone, but she also knew she couldn't be anything more for Damion. Neither of them was in a place for a relationship. He didn't want one, and she was starting to think she wasn't capable of one. However, she could fake it with him for a little while. "No, we don't need the pillow wall."

"Alright, well, come on and get in bed," he said.

She walked around the bed and cautiously got under the covers. She took the pillow and snuggled it up to her as she lay facing away from Damion. What had Paul been trying to say to her in the dream? It had been different from any of the others. Usually they were all nightmares, but this one had been happy for a few moments. It actually made the whole thing worse.

Naomi could feel the bed shift as Damion got in. He clicked the light and then pulled the covers up. He didn't move in close to her. Instead, he just reached out a hand and placed it on her back. The warmth of it was soothing. He had held her the whole night the night before and stayed true to his word. He didn't push her past anything she wasn't willing to do. Hell, he didn't even ask for anything.

"Damion," she whispered into the darkness.

"Yeah?" he whispered.

"Will you..." she started to say but then stopped.

"Will I what?" he asked.

She felt him shift again and knew he had turned toward her.

"Thank you for being so nice to me. I know this is weird," she said instead.

"Naomi, what were you going to ask?"

He didn't wait for a response. It was like he had read her mind. He moved in closer until he was close enough to pull her into him. His arms wrapped around her, and she could feel his warm breath on the back of her neck. He didn't say anything. He just held her while she cried. Her body was shaking, and his kindness meant more to her than she would ever be able to express.

She wasn't sure how long she lay there crying, but eventually the tears ran dry, and she felt her body relax. She knew Damion was still awake. His body was tense in a way that said he hadn't fallen asleep, but he hadn't spoken. He let her cry until she calmed.

"You don't have to thank me. I'm your friend, and I'm here for you," he finally whispered.

He shifted just a bit and gave her a soft kiss on her cheek before lying back down. For some reason, that small gesture made her smile. Warmth flooded her body. She knew this was dangerous. They were asking for trouble, but she couldn't help it. For the first time in five years, she felt peace. She felt cared about. She felt safe.

Chapter Eighteen

Naomi

It had been two weeks, and what started out as a little experiment had turned into a full-fledged friendship. Now and then, Damion went out, but he came back early and was ready to hang out as soon as he did. On those nights, Naomi would sit outside and enjoy nature. She loved being out in the forest, and with the sleep she was getting, she was actually able to enjoy it.

"Hey!" Damion called out, waving at her as he made his way up the road from the set. "I'm going to take a shower, but I got us something!"

"What?" she asked, trying to see what he had in his hand.

"Vodka!" he answered.

Naomi burst out laughing. She had been drinking vodka the night Damion had come to spend time with her. It was before he found out about everything and decided to commit to this very strange arrangement they had gotten entangled in.

"Okay, well I got something for you too!"

"Come over in ten minutes then?" he asked as he opened the door to his trailer. It was a similar scene to every night, but she didn't mind. Getting up, she went into her RV to clean herself up some and get her bag. While she had started spending almost every night over at Damion's, she never left things there. It was too presumptuous, and they were supposed to just be friends. The last thing she wanted was to make him think she was moving in on him.

Giving him fifteen minutes, she then made her way across the road with her bag and knocked on the door. Damion swung it open, and she walked in. They were so familiar at this point that it all seemed natural. She no longer got shy being there, and he seemed more relaxed. His hair was still wet, but he had put on his pajamas. Two glasses sat on his counter with a bottle of expensive vodka next to them.

"I see you don't like my discount swill."

"While I appreciate your choices, I thought we could do with something that wasn't going to eat our insides as it went down," he answered and poured two shots.

"So, are you trying to get me drunk tonight, or is there another reason for this?" she asked taking the shot.

They clinked their glasses together before throwing it back. The liquor was smoother, but still burned and she released a heavy breath when she was done swallowing.

"Neither. I just figured you might want something different tonight," he answered, taking the glass from her and filling them once more.

"I see," she answered and then took the next shot. Once she had downed it, she moved further into the trailer. "Do you have a hair dryer here?"

"No, I just let my hair dry on its own. Abby is the only one who uses that kind of stuff on me," he answered, giving her a suspicious look.

"Oh, okay, well, hold on. I'll be right back," Naomi answered and then went for the door. She ran across to her RV and grabbed her hair dryer and heat protectant spray. It probably wasn't as nice as what Abby would use, but it would work well enough.

When she returned, Damion gave her an arched look of curiosity. "What are you up to?"

"Trust me. Now sit down," she said.

He did as asked, and she plugged in her hair dryer. Getting his comb from the bathroom, she went about spraying his hair and drying it completely. His hair felt like silk, and she loved having her hands in it. Maybe this would give her an excuse to touch him more. Not that she should be touching him at all. However the more time they spent together, the harder it was to keep feelings from creeping in. He felt good, and he made her feel alive again after years in the darkness.

"Okay, my hair is dry. Now why did we dry it?" he asked, looking at her over his shoulder.

Naomi went to her bag and pulled out a black silk bonnet. Hers was pink, but she figured he would want a more manly color. "I told you I got you something. You can't put this on with wet hair," she said.

"You are not putting that on me." He laughed, turning and holding his hands out in front of him. He was so tall that it was easy for him to keep her away from him, but she wiggled through. Somehow, she ended up straddling his lap, but she was winning.

"Sit still. I promise it isn't going to hurt, and the only one who will know is me," she said and then went about putting the bonnet on him and tying it at the top of his forehead.

With her task finished, she realized the precarious position she had accidently put them in. Damion's hands were holding her at the hips to keep her from falling off of him, and she became very aware of just how close their bodies were. Her breath started to quicken, and she became a little dizzy. She should move. She should get up and go back to her RV. This was the line they were not supposed to cross.

Damion didn't seem to notice. Either that or he was proving to be an even better actor than she thought he was. "Woman, what have you done to me?" He gave her an incredulous look, and she looked down at him and started laughing.

Sliding off of his lap, she looked at him and let the more intense thoughts slide away to give way to her amusement at her handywork. "I put a bonnet on you. Your hair is now protected for when you sleep. Abby will notice. I promise."

"You really expect me to wear this all night?" he asked but didn't make a move to remove it.

"I do, and you are going to," she demanded.

"Okay, well, remember how I said I wasn't trying to get you drunk. Well now we are getting drunk for sure. That is the only way I'm going to be able to wear this all night," he said, but he laughed and got up to pour them each another shot.

"You won't be alone. I will have mine on too!" she defended.

Damion didn't find any comfort in that, but he just handed her a shot and turned on some music. "Drink, woman. Drink, and don't you dare take a picture of me."

"Oh, but I have to! I have to show Jessie!" Naomi exclaimed and grabbed her phone.

"You are not showing Jessie or anyone, for that matter. This stays between us." He reached for her hand before she could get the phone and pulled her to him. She smacked into his chest, and her breath caught as she got a strong whiff of his sandalwood scent.

It took a second for her to snap out of it, but she looked up at him and grinned. "You have to sleep sometime, and I know where you sleep."

"Just remember, I know where you sleep too," he said and then wrapped his arms around her and started dancing with her.

She vaguely remembered dancing with him the night he had found her drinking in the rain. That night was a bit of a wild blur, but she knew she had danced with him. Since then, they hadn't danced together, so being in that position once more had her head spinning.

The truth was, she was both terrified and tempted when she was around Damion. He was the first man to come into her life that made her think of doing anything beyond friendship. It was a bad idea, and up to that point they had managed to keep everything in the friend lane. But she was sure she could be convinced to change lanes. Maybe. That was where the fear came in. Would she ever be able to let go of Paul?

Her thoughts taking that darker turn, she moved away from Damion and went to sit on her side of the bed. She couldn't get closer to Damion. Even if he did want something from her, he would be competing with a ghost, and that was not fair to him.

"What happened? We were having fun, and now you're sad," Damion said, walking around the bed.

"Sorry, my mind just started thinking too much," she answered, taking a deep breath before looking up to him.

"Well stop. I look far too ridiculous for you to have that look," he answered and then gave a silly pose to show off his bonnet.

It made her laugh, and her fears slipped away again.

CHAPTER NINETEEN

DAMION

"We will be going to night shoots next week, so be ready to be up late. Adjust your schedule and we will pick up in a couple of days," the director said as they wrapped up for the day.

He had known night shoots were coming and had even talked to Naomi about the change in schedule. She seemed okay with everything and had gone over her plans to adjust to the new schedule. When she was working, she was extremely professional. When she wasn't working, she was lively and beautiful, funny and enchanting, and sad. No matter how silly or crazy their nights got, there was always moments where her mind drifted off and sadness took the place of laughter. He could do nothing to stop it, no matter how much he wished he could.

"Hey, Damion, what are you doing to your hair lately?" Abby asked, coming out of the makeup trailer.

"What do you mean?" he asked.

"I've been meaning to ask you for the last few days, but whatever you are doing is working. Your hair has looked amazing lately," she said then waved good-bye.

Naomi had won that one. She had managed to get him to put on the bonnet every night since getting it for him. Part of the reason he gave in was because it made her giggle, and he liked seeing her happy. Another reason for it was because she really wanted him to, and it was something he could do without compromising their relationship.

He couldn't count the number of cold showers he had taken since she had begun staying with him. While the pillow wall had gotten thrown out night one, so far, they hadn't broken any other rules. They always went to bed fully clothed, and there had been no touching that was anything beyond friendship, despite all his desire to push. Once or twice, he had woken up the way men tended to wake, and he had to shift from her to keep her from noticing. If she had, she certainly hadn't said anything.

"So, we have a couple of days off to change schedule. Do you want to come and entertain me some to keep me awake?" Allicia asked, walking up behind him.

Persistent as always. "You never give up."

"Look, you have been doing the best work of your life lately, and when you kiss me, you have to admit something is there. Let me show you just how much." She moved in close to him and ran her hand up his body into his hair. She lifted up on her toes and moved in to kiss him, but he stepped away. As much as he could use some relief from his torment, Allicia was not the one he would go to for it. Giving in to her would just complicate an already complicated situation.

"I don't think that's a good idea. Thank you for the compliment, but I'm not interested, and you know that," he answered as he moved away from her.

"Why? You aren't seeing anyone else. I know you aren't. So why not give it a try? Hell, we all know how much of a slut you can be when you want to," she protested, grabbing his hand and pulling him back to her. "Just come back to my trailer, and we can drink and fuck. You'll see just how much you've missed it."

"No," he said, his voice firm and cold.

"What the hell is going on with you? We have hooked up several times since we broke up. Why is this different?" she asked.

"It just is," he answered. "Look, I have to go. My dinner is going to get cold."

"Fine, whatever. See you on Monday," she growled and stormed off.

Naomi was stepping out of Maria's trailer by the time he got there, and he smiled seeing her. She must have been dropping off dinner to Maria as she did every night. "Hey! I was thinking we could eat dinner sitting out in front of my RV. It's a nice night."

When she said it was a nice night, she meant it was overcast with a bit of a cool breeze. The weather had turned uncomfortably hot over the last week, and there was a forecast for rain. Everyone had been staying inside as much as possible to avoid the horrible heat and humidity Georgia offered in the summer.

"That sounds like a good idea. Oh,.. you win one."

"Win one what?" she asked, falling into step next to him.

"Abby said my hair is looking better. She asked me what I have been doing," he answered.

Naomi laughed, and the sound filled him with warmth. "Did you tell her?"

"Hell no! Do you think I'm crazy?" he said.

Naomi didn't stop at the kitchen. Instead, they went straight to her RV. She had an ice chest sitting outside with several citronella tiki torches burning to keep the bugs at bay. "Take a seat. I put the food inside until we got here. I didn't want bugs getting into it."

"Smart," he said and took a seat. While he waited, he opened up the ice chest and pulled out a diet soda. She had a mix of sodas, water, and alcohol inside to give him options. Naomi was always good at giving options.

"So I did something different tonight. It isn't quite on plan for you, but I think it will be okay," she said as she came out of the RV holding two plates. He wondered if she waited tables when she was younger with how comfortable she was at holding plates and trays. He realized he hadn't asked too much about her past, knowing most of it was painful for her.

"What do you mean different?" he asked, getting up to help.

"So, I made some grilled cheeseburgers. I wrapped them in giant lettuce leaves so you don't have a bun, and then I made some beet chips. I know they're carbs, but beets are a vegetable and very good for you," she answered.

He looked down at his plate and grinned. "This is perfect. Thank you."

They ate, and when their food was done, she put the plates inside. Then they sat there enjoying the night air while drinking and talking.

He told her about his day, even going into detail about his argument with Allicia. "It's getting to where I may not be able to work with her anymore. She just won't take no for an answer."

"Well, do you blame her? You two have history, and you haven't really given her any reason not to do stuff together. Actually, what is your reason?" she asked, surprising him.

He often questioned whether the attraction between them was one-sided, and when she asked questions like that it made him think it was.

"I'm too old to just mess around with people. One-night stands is one thing, but that isn't what she wants. I'm not going to lead her on," he answered. He hadn't been having sex at all since the night he found Naomi drunk in the rain.

"You sound like a completely different person from when we first became friends," she said, but he noticed a tone in her voice he couldn't read.

Thunder echoed out, and a moment later the heavens opened up and started pouring down on them. They were under the awning so remained dry, but it was a hard, loud rain all the same. Naomi got up and turned up the radio before coming to sit down again. They had stayed to water and soda, so there was no alcohol between them. But he couldn't help but think of that night when he found her drunk off her ass and desperately sad. It had been so perfect in all its imperfections. For a few drunken hours, they were just happy and being silly. It wasn't often he got to be that way, but with Naomi, he had found it happening more often than not.

"I love the rain," she said, looking out into the night. The water had made the tiki torches go out, so it was much darker than it had been before.

"Why is that?" he asked. He had assumed she enjoyed the rain with how she had acted before, but she'd never said.

"I always have. Paul and I, we used to play in the rain, dance in the rain. It just felt so..." she stopped as if she didn't have the words to describe what she was trying to say.

"Free," he said for her.

She turned and looked at him, the bottle of soda she had been drinking resting at her lips. "Yeah, free."

Silence fell between them after that, and they sat comfortably listening to the mix of music and rain. Every so often he would look over at her and wonder what she was thinking. Her brow was creased, and he knew she was deep in thought, but he wouldn't push her to say anything. He was fine just sitting there and enjoying the night.

A song came on, and he remembered it as the song they danced to before. He wasn't sure if it was pushing for him to do it, but he got up and held his hand out to her. "Come dance with me."

She blinked a couple of times and then a smile slowly spread over her lips. She set down her bottle and took his hand. Within seconds he had dragged her out into the freezing cold rain and pulled her close to him so they could dance. He held one hand in his and his other rested at the small of her back as they swayed together. The rain poured over them, soaking them through in moments, but neither of them seemed to care. She had her spare hand resting on his chest, and he wished he didn't have a shirt on so he could feel it on his skin.

They danced from one song into the next. It was a faster song, but they didn't speed up. They continued to sway, slow and steady, oblivious to the world around them. It was the single most passionate moment of his life, and he couldn't stop himself. He could no longer hold back.

"Naomi," he whispered, pulling her as close to him as possible.

"Yes?" she asked, her voice shaking.

"I want to kiss you," he said, holding his breath.

He never had to ask. Women always threw themselves at him, but Naomi was different. She wasn't like the other women he had dallied with. He didn't want to dally with her. He wanted to kiss her and hold her. She made him want things he never had before.

"No," she answered, and pain filled his heart. For a second, he thought of walking away, but he couldn't.

They continued to dance as one song played into the next. His question hadn't ruined the mood, but her body was more tense. What was going on in that head of hers? Getting brave, he decided to try again. "Naomi."

"Yes?" she asked in a repeat of the last time.

It took him a second to actually get the words out, but he managed. "I want to kiss you."

This time she didn't say anything. At least not at first. She looked up at him, and they stopped moving. The pounding of his heart took the place of the storm around him. She licked the water off of her lips, and just the sight of her tongue on her lips sent a shot of electricity down his spine. Time stood still as he waited for her to respond.

"Yes," she said, and he held back no more.

He crashed his lips against hers and kissed her with every ounce of pent-up passion he had inside of him.

CHAPTER TWENTY

NAOMI

She had never kissed anyone else, and it had been more than five years since her last kiss. Damion kissed people all the time. Hell, part of his job was kissing. So when she said yes, and he took her mouth with his, she was overwhelmed. He kissed her like he was starving, and it stole her breath and made her dizzy. She had to pull away.

"Damion," she gasped, not sure what the hell they were doing.

"I'm sorry. I had to kiss you," he said, his hands moving into her hair as he rested his forehead against hers.

"I just. I don't know what to do," she said. Even her words weren't coming easily for her. She was filled with a mix of terror and desire, and she had no idea which was going to win.

"You're fine. Just..." he licked his lips, and this time she was the one to start.

She moved in and pressed her lips to his. He didn't ravish her mouth like he had before. Instead, he took things easier, kissing her with care. Slowly she opened her mouth to him, and he entered her, his tongue teasing hers for a moment before they got lost in just the motion of their lips working together. The rain poured down harder, but nothing was distracting them from it. They kissed there in the rain for what seemed like an eternity.

Then Damion did the unexpected. He grabbed her by the ass and picked her up. She had to wrap her legs around him to keep from falling as he carried her toward his trailer. The whole way they stayed lost in the kiss. Her heart was racing, making her more and more dizzy with every passing second. When they got to the trailer, he threw the door open, and the two of them stumbled in, but he didn't drop her or stop kissing her the whole time. Slamming the door closed, he pushed her against it and continued to feed from her lips.

She moaned and an almost pain-filled groan escaped his throat before he started to take his kisses from her lips down her throat. He lapped up the water that dripped down her as he kissed and sucked along the sensitive flesh. One of his hands was still on her butt, keeping her lifted against him and the other was tangled in her hair. What started out as a kiss was quickly progressing, and she wasn't sure if she wanted to stop or push it further.

Damion made his way back to her lips, and they got lost in kissing once more. She could feel his body reacting to her. It was impossible not to notice with how tightly he was pressed to her. Her body was reacting, and that terrified her more than the kissing did. She sank her fingers into his silky hair and put her focus into kissing him back. He wasn't pressuring her for more than that, and the way he kissed her made her feel alive.

When he broke the kiss to trail down the other side of her neck, his body pushed forward, and the pressure made her almost cry out. Need was taking over. Powerful, starving need wanted her to give in to what had been building between the two of them for weeks. "Damion," she said, her voice coming out breathy.

"Yes?" he asked between kisses.

What the hell was she going to say? Do more? Stop? She couldn't breathe through the growing passion. It was more intense than she had ever fantasized about back in her teenage years. Never had she thought he would feel like this.

When she didn't answer, he stopped kissing her but stayed pressed up against her. He rested his head against hers and held her close.

"Naomi?" he said her name like it was a question. He would stop if she asked him to. She knew without a doubt that he would.

"Sit down on the bed," she said, and he wasted no time.

He didn't put her down to take her to the bed. He held her tightly and made his way into the room until he was sitting on the bed. Once he was seated, she ran her hands down either side of him and took hold of his shirt. She had it pulled halfway up when he stopped her.

"I won't push you into anything you don't want to do," he said, his eyes looking deeply into hers.

"I know," she answered and finished pulling his shirt off.

She tossed it behind her, and it plopped down with a thud. Then she grabbed her own shirt and pulled it over her head, tossing it to join his. Damion's eyes moved from her face down her body, and he let his hands slowly glide up her sides. She still had on her bra, but it was the most skin she had ever shown him. He reached up and took hold of the ring she wore around her neck.

He held it for just a moment before letting it go and looking up at her. For those few short seconds, Naomi thought about pulling away, but she didn't. Gently he trailed his fingers over her skin, tracing each muscle and curve as if he were trying to memorize it.

"You are so beautiful," he whispered before wrapping around her again, kissing her hard and deep.

The kisses grew more and more passionate the longer they continued, but when they stopped next it was because of her. She took a turn, exploring him with her mouth and tongue. She kissed and licked along his jaw, the tickle of his five o'clock shadow teasing her as she moved. Then she nibbled against his earlobe, and his hands tightened around her as the most intoxicating sound escaped him. He leaned back some, using one hand to keep him from falling completely back, but it gave her the angle she needed to explore his neck and chest with her mouth and tongue. His breath grew more and more heavy as she explored, and more soft moans echoed out of him.

His grip on her hip grew tighter, and then he lifted his hips up against her a bit so a shock of pleasure burst over her. It was only a teasing sensation but more than she had felt in a long time. Then he took hold of her and flipped them over.

He laid her down on the bed and took his time exploring what parts of her body she had exposed to him. He didn't pull her bra away or pop open the button of her jeans, but if it was exposed, he touched it, kissed it, nibbled it. Her body arched and moved with every ounce of attention he gave to it, hungry for touch in a way she hadn't realized she needed until that moment.

"Oh god!" she cried out when he managed to get a bite to her hip bone. How had he been able to reach? Then she remembered her jeans were loose and she was wiggling around a lot.

"Fuck, baby," he whispered before finding her lips again. He growled into the kiss, his arm wrapping around her as he lifted her again, pushing her higher up on the bed so they weren't halfway hanging off anymore, but he kept his lips and tongue dancing with hers. It was as if his hands and his lips were capable of doing two different things all at once. She didn't feel as talented, her focus solely on kissing and touching him.

He pulled her legs up on either side of his hips and then pushed forward. The hardness of him rubbed against her in such a way that another burst of pleasure erupted from every nerve in her body, and she arched back with a cry. He used that position to kiss and lick along her throat down along her collar bone then back to her chin. He pushed against her again, and she began to tremble.

He took hold of her hair and turned her to look into his eyes. "Tell me to stop and I will," he said before kissing her again.

They shouldn't have even started, but now that they had, she didn't want to stop. They moved together, kissing and touching like teenagers. She could feel his need, and her own grew higher and higher. It was torture, but she wasn't ready for more. She hadn't even realized she was ready for this. His mouth, his hands, everything felt so good, tasted heavenly. Despite still being mostly dressed, the motion of their bodies was building up a pressure she hadn't felt in far too long. A part of her deep inside wanted to stop it, but she couldn't. She needed it.

Their kisses got more and more ravenous the faster their bodies rolled together, and before she realized what was happening, her head flung back, and she screamed out into the darkness of the room as her body shook and writhed in an explosion of pleasure. Her legs tightened around him, holding him tightly to her as she let the sensation roll in waves over her. The kissing had stopped, and she realized he was watching her.

When the intensity wore off, heat rose on her cheeks, and she suddenly felt extremely embarrassed, but Damion didn't let that last. He cupped her cheek and gave sweet soft kisses along the crease of her mouth. "So beautiful. I could watch you like that all night," he whispered between each kiss.

She knew he was still ready for more, and she started to reach down between them, but he stopped her. "No, not yet. I just want to kiss you." So he did. They kissed and touched all night, never removing any more clothes.

Eventually exhaustion took the place of passion, and they collapsed in each other's arms panting. He had made her feel so much pleasure that she was trembling. Never once did he push for more, even though she knew he wanted it. He just held her and gave to her. It was sweet, romantic, and oh so terrifying.

Chapter Twenty-One

Damion

His whole body throbbed. The one time she had moved to take care of him in the same way he had her, he stopped her. She wasn't ready for that step, and no matter how badly he had wanted to take her body and show her just how deeply he wanted her, he stopped her so she could process one thing at a time. It didn't stop him from giving it all to her. When he had heard that first moan escapes her when he had pressed into her, all he wanted was to make it happen again and again, so that was exactly what he did. He kissed her, touched her, and made her body feel pleasure without the pressure of having to give back.

Sure, it made him completely unable to sleep, and he was more than certain that a cold shower was not going to cure him this time, but it had been worth it. His lips were swollen from kissing her, and his room was filled with the scent of her skin and desire. It was intoxicating. Reaching down, he adjusted himself again and then turned and kissed the top of her head.

His biggest fear was she would wake up and regret everything they had done. It was why he had stopped them from going all the way. Kissing was one thing, but if he had made love to her, there was no going back. He didn't want to give himself to her and then her hate him for it after. It was far too easy to get lost in passion when you were in the middle of it, but the problem was it wasn't just passion for him. He was falling for her, hard and deep, and it made him want to guard himself.

She moaned a bit and snuggled in closer, but she was still asleep. He had watched her all night. At one moment she had woken up for just a few minutes and kissed along his chest, but he had petted her back to sleep. No way could he do make-out session two without giving in to more. The rules of their arrangement were shattering, and he knew it was a terrible idea. He just didn't care.

This girl had come out of nowhere and changed everything about him. They both had been broken in their own ways, but he was starting to think she might be the only one he was willing to fix himself for. The problem was, he wasn't sure she felt the same way.

Another half hour went by before Naomi finally woke up. She moaned softly and wiggled a bit before turning to look up at him. Her hair was a mess, having dried while they had been making out. No way would a bonnet be fixing that. However, she still was the most beautiful woman he had ever seen.

"Morning," he whispered and petted her hair away from her face.

Several expressions crossed her face before she finally answered him. "Morning, ummm, we... well," she stuttered as if unable to find the words. Was she angry? Was she happy? What was about to change between the two of them?

"We kissed, a lot," he said, prompting her to move past her embarrassment.

"Yeah, we did," she said and smiled, a light pink coming to her cheeks.

Strangely, that smile relieved some of the fear and tension he had building up in him. She wasn't yelling at him or pushing him away. Then she shifted and moved to sit on his lap. Damn, no he was not prepared for this. His hands found her hips, and he did a half sit-up to meet her as she leaned in to kiss him again. His tender lips begged for her kiss, and he wrapped around her to savor every second of it.

"What are we doing?" she asked, pulling away just enough to speak.

"Kissing," he answered, nipping at her lips a bit.

"I know, but what are we doing?" she asked again but they ended up kissing instead.

They made out for several more minutes before she pulled all the way away from him and sat up on him. Fuck if she didn't look sexy as hell straddling his lap, half naked in his bed.

"This is crazy, you know."

"Yeah, it is, but..." he couldn't look at her as he continued to talk. It would break him if he saw her rejection. Instead, he traced his fingers over her tummy and sides as he continued. "I want you, Naomi. I know that we are very different, and we both have our own issues, but I want to be with you."

"Damion..." she said, her voice shaky. Silence filled the room for a second, and then she took his hands in hers. "I'm scared."

That made him look up at her. She wasn't telling him to leave her alone. She wasn't saying they couldn't pursue this, whatever it was. All she said was she was afraid, which was something he could handle because it didn't mean she didn't want him.

"It's okay to be scared." He brushed his thumb across her cheek before taking hold of her and rolling her back onto the bed. He leaned up on his elbow so he could look at her. "You've been through a lot, and I'm not going to pretend to know what it felt like. I don't want to take the place of your past. I just want to be with you, and we can do that as slowly or fast as you want. I'll always stop if you tell me to."

He stroked her cheek and then leaned down to kiss her softly. It wasn't the passion-filled kiss of the night before, but it was full of meaning.

She cupped his cheeks as they kissed and then smiled when he pulled away. "I can't make any promises," she said.

"I'm not asking you to. We can take this one moment at a time. Okay?" he answered.

"Yeah, I can do that," she said.

They kissed again, but she insisted on getting up. He reminded her of the change of schedule and let her know he was going to try and get some rest. She told him she was going to get some things done in the kitchen and that he could find her there later. He hoped that after she left, she didn't come to her senses and tell him they shouldn't kiss anymore. The moment she was gone, all he wanted was to get her back and kiss her again.

Instead, he got up and made his way to his shower. He tried a cold shower, but it didn't help. Ultimately, he found himself having to relieve his own stress, but she had given him lots to think about while he did. Finally relaxed, he went to bed and fell asleep wrapped in the scent of her where it had soaked into his sheets.

CHAPTER TWENTY-TWO

NAOMI

"Jessie, I have no idea what I'm doing," Naomi said as she chopped up the vegetables for Damion's dinner later.

After leaving Damion's trailer, all she could think about was how distracted she had gotten with him. They shouldn't have kissed. They sure as hell shouldn't have made out, and the things he made her body feel, well that was as far from the plan as it could get. If Naomi knew what was good for her, she would be running, but she didn't want to. She felt like a human again when she was with him. The fear, the pain, it all just slipped away when they talked and laughed. For those moments in time, the past didn't exist, but a relationship with him was insane.

"You mean to tell me, you actually got your hands on Damion Malcom, and you don't know what to do? Girl, don't take this the wrong way, but get your ass cleaned up, buy some new underwear, and go for it," Jessie answered. They were on a video call, and she could see her friend leaning back on the couch and laughing at her.

"Are you crazy?" Naomi protested, looking up from the cutting board. "He's my boss."

"Who you have been sleeping with for weeks and have had a crush on since you were a teenager. Look, I know it's hard for you because of everything that happened, but it's time. Stop calling me and being wishy washy about him and just do it. You will feel so much better," Jessie explained.

Naomi could feel herself blushing, and it embarrassed her even more. Jessie had been telling her it was time to move on for a couple of years now, but this was the first time Naomi had done anything close to that. Logically, Naomi knew it was well past the mourning phase, and she should let go, but logic had nothing to do with emotions, and she had been holding on to Paul with everything she had.

"Jessie, it isn't that easy."

"Look, the two of you call me all the time with your 'should I' and 'shouldn't Is,' so this is me telling you: Yes, you should. Damn, the boy already gave you an orgasm, now let him give you a proper one," Jessie said.

Naomi nearly cut herself when Jessie said that. She hadn't quite admitted to herself that what Damion had done to her was an orgasm, but Jessie didn't seem to have a problem putting it out there for the universe to hear. "Jessie, someone could walk in."

"I don't care. I am very pregnant and uncomfortable, so I'm going to take it out on you. Look, I know you are never going to fully let go of Paul, and you shouldn't. No one forgets their first anyway, and while Paul was way more than that, he would have been with you no matter what. No one is saying to let go of that, but even he wouldn't want you torturing yourself like this. He's dead, and he isn't coming back. Damion is very much alive and giving you a side of himself he has never given to anyone else. Don't take it for granted because you are holding on to a shadow."

Jessie's blunt words nearly cut her in half. For several moments, Naomi didn't know what to say. She stood there, holding the knife above the half-cut carrot and staring off into nothing, lost in thought. Then she snapped back into it. "I need to go to town."

"Yeah, you do. Now get to it. I'm going to find a snack and then get a nap," Jessie said. They said their good-byes and then Naomi went back to her kitchen duties.

When the door to the kitchen swung open, Naomi jumped and squealed, her thoughts having taken over her perception. "Whoa, didn't mean to scare you," Damion said as he came in to steady her.

He stood there for a moment then leaned in and kissed her. It was just a soft kiss, and then he pulled back and smiled at her. All of her ability to be a normal human had flown out of the window. She took a deep breath and then blurted out. "What's your favorite color?"

Damion looked back at her, confused and a bit shocked, before answering, "Green, why?"

"I just wanted to know. I, umm, I'm almost done getting everything set up here. Then I need to go to town. Do you need me to pick up anything for you?" she asked and then turned to finish tossing everything into the skillet to sauté. She was making a quick stir fry with cauliflower rice for him. It was easy, and when she made it the last time, he had really enjoyed it.

"I can't think of anything, but are you okay?" he asked, following her around the kitchen a bit as she worked.

"Yeah, I'm fine. Sorry, my head is just spinning some. I talked to Jessie a bit and she got me all flustered," Naomi answered.

"Is everything okay with her? Is the baby, okay?" Damion asked, concern entering his tone.

"Oh, yeah, she is fine. She was just, well you know... Jessie. She can be pretty direct. Anyway, here is your food. I will see you in a little while," she said, managing to turn off everything before shoving a plate in Damion's direction.

She gave him a quick kiss and then walked out of the kitchen trailer.

Going into town to get "ready" for Damion was easier said than done, and it hadn't been easy to begin with. First, she went to the lingerie store to get new underclothes. It had been a while since she got anything fancy and was out of her element as she looked through the racks. Finally, a girl came over to help her and guided her to something she felt was fitting for her.

It was black and emerald green. The panties were bikini cut and the top was a sort of fancy bra that then had a sheer layer hanging from it. It was pretty and wasn't so sexy that she would feel uncomfortable. The steps between celibate and going to bed with self-proclaimed man whore were many, but she could take one or two in his direction.

After picking out her outfit for the night, she got a few matching sets in case she needed something in the future. Naomi couldn't help feeling a bit presumptuous doing all of this, but Jessie had never steered her wrong before. Nervous as she was, she knew her friend was right.

With the clothes purchased, she then went to take care of the rest of her. She got a mani-pedi and then braved the waxing chair. Once she was smooth and pampered, she finished off with making sure she had plenty of her jasmine perfume. Damion always made comments about it, and she knew he really like it. Lately she had been using it sparingly because she was running low, but for Damion, she wanted to make sure she had plenty on hand.

CHAPTER TWENTY-THREE

DAMION

She had left him standing there with a plate of food and a messy kitchen. Damion wasn't really sure what to make of it, but he knew who would know. Taking a seat at the table, he dialed Jessie's number and waited for her to answer.

"I will tell you what I told her. Fuck and get it over with. I'm trying to take a nap," Jessie said without even a hello.

"What?" he asked, not sure he had actually heard those words come out of his friend and former chef's mouth.

"I spent half the morning on the phone with Naomi. I know all about the late night make-out session. The two of you call me all the time talking about how you feel and don't want to feel for each other. Get over it. It's time for you two to get on with it," she explained.

"You told this to Naomi?" he asked, so distracted by the conversation that he wasn't even tasting his food.

"Maybe not quite as crudely as I did with you, but yes. I told her to go to town, get cleaned up, buy some new underwear, and get on with it. You two like each other, but she is stuck in the past, and you are trying to convince yourself that you don't want a relationship. The truth of the matter is, the moment you asked her to stay the night with you, good intentions or not, it was over. So, fuck her and move forward. She needs it, you need it, and it will do both of you some good," Jessie explained.

Damion took a moment to process it all. He hadn't realized they were both going to Jessie and keeping her in the middle of things. It actually made him feel guilty, but it was too late. "You sure she wants to do that?"

"Damion, that girl is never going to be ready until someone nudges her in that direction. She is going to hold on to that ghost with everything she has because Paul is all she has ever known. I'd like to think you are man enough to understand that she will always hold on to him but can also develop something with you. Don't tell me you are too chicken to step up," Jessie was poking at the situation, stirring it up to make it go somewhere.

"I don't want to scare her away," he answered.

"Did she run last night?" Jessie asked.

"No," he answered.

"Well, there you go. Now, I had my snack and I'm going to take a nap. Find something to do with yourself and then be ready because you are going to need it tonight," Jessie said, laughing a bit.

How the hell was he supposed to get through a whole day with the thought that Naomi may want to actually take him to bed in a sexual way for the first time. Deciding he needed to stay busy to keep his mind off of all the delicious thoughts his imagination was stirring up, he went about cleaning the kitchen.

He had never done a lot of cleaning, and the task turned out to be far more difficult than he expected, but it did keep him busy. By the time he finished, it was time for him to go to a production meeting.

They weren't going to start the night shoots until Monday, but they were going to be going over some of the logistics and rehearsing some of the more difficult scenes in the meantime.

Maria was waiting for him just outside of her trailer, and when she looked up at him, her face grew hard and angry. "What the fuck did you do?"

"Nice to see you too. Everyone is being so aggressive with me today," he answered, avoiding actually answering her question.

"Right," Maria said sardonically. "I'll ask again. What the fuck did you do?"

He stopped and turned to look at her. He knew this was going to happen, and he'd rather it happen near her trailer than in ear range of the rest of the cast a crew. "I kissed Naomi."

Before saying something, Maria reached up and popped him on the back of his head. "What happened to the whole being friends and the arrangement is platonic BS?"

"It was until it wasn't. Look, I'm well aware how bad of an idea all of this is, but she makes me feel things. Maria, I have never felt like this before," he tried to explain.

Maria's eyebrow shot up and an almost sneer curled up on her lips, "What are you saying? Are you falling in love with her?"

Having it laid out in front of him made it more difficult to think about than he had anticipated. Love was a big step for him. He had shoved the idea of it away for so long that he thought it would never happen, but when Maria asked, he knew the truth.

Sometime between that night in the rain and the make-out session Damion had fallen in love with Naomi. He wasn't sure he was ready to say it, but he knew deep down it was the truth.

"I care a lot about her, and we have gotten close," he answered. Absentmindedly he started patting on his shirt and pants, looking for a cigarette. Over the last several weeks he had all but quit, not wanting to smell like smoke when Naomi was around him, but he suddenly found himself in desperate need of a smoke.

"What are you doing?" Maria asked.

"I need a cigarette. Like I really need one," he said.

"Don't look at me. I don't smoke, and you told me you were quitting.

"Damn it!" Damion exclaimed and then saw one of the crew members with a cigarette. Walking over, he asked the guy to bum one, and the other man handed over what was left of his pack along with a lighter.

"I have another pack in my bag. You can have that one," the man said then turned back to his work.

Damion was shaking as he brought the cigarette to his lips and lit it. He sucked in a deep inhale and held it for several seconds before letting it go. The relaxing sensation of it traveled over every nerve in his body as he slowly exhaled before taking another drag. He savored it for several moments before heading toward the set.

Maria didn't push about his life choices after that. Instead, they focused on work. Damion smoked two cigarettes before making it to the production meeting. They were there for a couple of hours before breaking.

"Maria, can I borrow your shower?" he asked on the way back. Only one more cigarette was left in the pack, so he indulged it, knowing it was going to hinder the progress he had made in quitting.

"Why do you need my shower?" she asked.

"I don't want to go to my trailer smelling like smoke. It will linger in there," he answered as if that made all the sense in the world.

"So, you want to make *my* trailer smell like smoke?" she asked sarcastically, but she motioned for him to join her. "Just be quick about it. I have an extra toothbrush in there too if you need it," Maria explained pointing him in the direction of the shower.

"You are a life saver. Thank you," he said, kissing her cheek.

"This is not me approving of your decision. I just also know I can't stop you, so I might as well take out as many of the ways for this to go wrong as possible," she said.

Maria was right and had been from the start. Getting involved with Naomi was not the smartest of ideas, but he couldn't stop himself. Maria had said the truth earlier, and even if he couldn't say it, he knew it deep down. He had fallen for Naomi.

CHAPTER TWENTY-FOUR

NAOMI

She had no idea what she was doing. How had Jessie convinced her to do this. Damion had been in some sort of meeting when Naomi got back from town, and she had snuck into his trailer to set things up. For all she knew, he didn't want to actually have sex with her, but she had committed to the idea and was going to follow through no matter how awkward and terrifying it was.

The first thing she did was straighten things up in the room and light some candles. After seeing how cheesy she had made it, she blew out the candles and just left the light on. The room being cleaned up was good enough. Then she went into the bathroom to change into her new outfit. It fit her well, but she couldn't help feeling awkward at dressing up. The girl at the store had taken her measurements to make sure they got the right size, and regardless of her nerves, Naomi was pleased with how well it actually fit was. She had thought she would look slutty in it, but she didn't. Instead, she felt sexy, cute, and shy.

Paul's ring still hung from the necklace she wore, but she thought it would be too awkward for them. So for the first time in five years, she took it off. Not knowing what to do with it, she put it in a small box Damion had on the bathroom counter. The last thing she wanted was for it to get washed down the drain on accident.

She had just finished combing her hair and freshening her breath when she heard Damion come in. Before she had invaded his trailer, she had sent him a text to let him know she was back and would be coming over. It was go time, so why did she feel frozen?

"Naomi?" Damion asked from the main room.

"I'll, ummm, be right out," she called from the bathroom.

When she didn't head right out, Damion tapped on the door. "Are you okay in there?" he asked.

"Yes, I'm fine. I'm just..." Nervous as hell? No, she couldn't tell him that. She had decided this was what she was doing, and there was no backing out now. "Can you turn off the overhead light?"

"Sure," Damion answered, his voice sounding curious.

When she saw the light dim from the crack under the door, she knew there was no more waiting. Taking a deep breath, she slowly opened the bathroom door. Damion was dressed as he often was when he wasn't working in jeans and a T-shirt. His hair was damp, and he had combed it back with his fingers. How could he look so normal and calm when she felt like she might faint from anxiety?

Pushing the door the rest of the way open, she stepped out and stood there while Damion stared. His eyes ran up and down her body several times before he moved toward her. He didn't say anything, and she had desperately hoped he would. Instead, he pulled her to him and kissed her, soft and sweet, but deep. They kissed for several moments before he pulled away and guided her toward the bed. Taking a seat, he let himself gaze over her body before he spoke. "You look so fucking hot right now. Did you do this for me?"

She felt the blush instantly and tried to hide, but he pulled her hand away and kissed the inside of her palm. "I did. I wanted to look pretty for you," she answered. She had also hoped it would make her feel more confident. It didn't.

"You always look pretty, and you don't ever have to do anything special for me. That said, I do appreciate it. This is lovely. You are lovely," she could feel his fingers trembling as he traced over the edges of her outfit, touching her skin but tempting what was covered. "Are you sure you want to do this?"

No, she wasn't sure of anything, but she wasn't going to say that. Jessie was right. It was past time for her to move on. "I want to do this."

He reached up and pulled her to him, wrapping around her and kissing her hard and deep. His ravenous kiss stole her breath, and she wanted more. They kissed like that for several moments before he pulled away.

"Naomi, listen to me. I want to say this before we go any further, okay?"

"Okay," she answered, panting after the heated kiss.

"If at any point you want me to stop, tell me. I don't want to fuck things up. I care about you, and I want you, but that also means doing things at your pace. So, promise me you will tell me to stop if you want me to because I can't promise I will remember to ask again," he said, holding her gaze. His words were as serious as the look in his eyes, and she found herself smiling.

"I promise I will tell you if I need to stop," she answered.

He didn't say anything else. He resumed kissing her. There was more hunger, more desire in the way he kissed her than he even had the night before. It was raw and intense, and proved he had been holding back. With her permission, he let go of some of that control, and she could sense it right away.

She pulled off his shirt so she could get her hands against the heat of his skin. She loved how hot and hard his muscles were and loved to feel him moving under her fingers. This time he pushed the boundaries she had left. Instead of kissing around the fabric, Damion pulled the straps of her top down and lowered the fabric until her breasts were free to him. He made a hiss of appreciation and then captured a nipple in his mouth, sucking and nibbling it a bit to create a mix of pleasure and pain that had her gasping. Her back arched, and he splayed his hand wider to support her. While he continued to give one breast attention, he used his other hand to cup and massage her other one. His hands were almost big enough to take her whole breast in one but not quite.

"You taste so good. I want to taste more of you," he whispered next to her ear. He unsnapped and removed her top, tossing it away before he stood up and laid her down on the bed.

He popped open the button of his jeans but didn't take them off. She was confused at first, but then he moved between her legs, lifting her hips to pull away the fabric of her panties, and her mind could no longer focus on anything but the attention he was giving her.

A mix of excitement and shyness raced through her as he exposed the rest of her body. She was naked, and he was still half dressed. Then he lifted her legs over his shoulders. She didn't know what he was doing until he was lying between her legs.

His lips explored up and down each inner thigh, and then he spread her open wide and gave her one long deep lick to the most sensitive part of her body. Her insecurities faded away as he took her into his mouth, licking, sucking, and exploring her with fervor. He shifted so he could use his fingers and open her up for him, and he found that spot that made her head spin. Her breaths came hard and heavy as he built that pressure up in her body, getting her close to the tipping point before easing off just enough to keep her waiting.

She wasn't sure she wanted to wait, but the torture was delicious. He brought her to that edge over and over. She looked down the line of her body to watch him and nearly screamed when he looked up at her with eyes so full of lust that it stunned her.

"Let go for me, baby," he whispered and then took to her savagely, building her higher and higher until she couldn't hold on anymore.

Her fingers sank into his hair as she arched into him. A vicious scream came from her as her body exploded in pleasure. If she had thought it felt good the night before, that was nothing compared to this moment. As she released, he continued to push her, making her orgasm roll one after another until she was pushing him away from her.

A soft chuckle escaped him as he kissed his way up her body until he found her lips. She could taste herself on his lips, which made her moan deeply into the kiss.

"That was the sexiest thing I have ever seen in my life," he growled against her lips. His hand ran down her body and then slowly began to play between her legs.

"Don't you want me to touch you too?" she asked, turning him to look at her.

"God yes, I do, but first, I want to make sure you are very ready for me," he explained.

It wasn't like she was a virgin, but he was certainly treating her like one. "What do you mean?"

"Naomi, I know it has been a long time for you. I want to just make sure you really enjoy this. Okay? Now, let me make you feel good," he answered and then sank a finger deep inside her. Her legs fell open wider, and she arched up into his attention, no longer caring about the conversation. "So fucking tight."

He leaned down and kissed her again as he slowly pushed his finger in and out of her before adding a second. He used his hand to loosen up her body and then curved his fingers just right to hit that special spot deep inside. His slow motions grew faster and more purposeful. He held his lips just above hers as she began to pant and gasp. Her hands fisted into the sheets as her hips started to roll in time to his attention.

"Yes, that's it, baby. Take all the pleasure you want from me."

She started to respond, but he hit that spot one more time. Her head flung back, and she screamed out as another intense orgasm coursed through her body. It wasn't fair. He was making her feel so good. He held himself right above her, his lips so close to hers that she could feel his breath on hers, but not kissing her.

"Yes, that's it. Oh, you feel so good, baby."

He let her ride out every aftershock before kissing her again. She pressed herself to him with everything she had, and she could feel him rocking his hips. That was it. She needed to give back some too. She reached between them and slipped her hand into his pants. He started to pull away, but she used her leg to hold him to her.

Her hand rubbed against his length, and the warm velvety sensation of him was accompanied by a slight throbbing against her palm. Then she wrapped her fingers around him and began to stroke him. His pants were in the way, and he seemed to realize that. He used one hand to push the fabric away and the other to hold himself up. His hips thrust against her motion, and he was now in the position she had been in moments ago. His look spoke of desire, pleasure, and wanting, and she knew that was all for her.

She kept up her attention on him, savoring the sounds he made as he moved with her. She watched his body and how it reacted. His stomach contracted in time with the strokes she gave him, and his whole-body trembled as he tried to hold on. She didn't want him to hold on. She wanted him to feel what he had made her feel.

Instead, he pulled away, gasping for air before stepping off the bed for a second. He finished removing his pants and then climbed back on top of her and kissed her.

"Naomi," he whispered against her lips.

"Yes," she answered breathlessly.

"Are you sure?" he asked one last time, and in response, she spread her legs open wider and pulled him closer to her.

It was all the answer he needed. He kissed her, hard and deep, and pushed himself slowly inside of her. He took his time as if to keep from hurting her, but once he was completely inside of her, she found herself clinging to him.

"You okay?" he asked, petting her hair from her face and kissing her softly.

"Yes, I'm fine," she answered and then leaned up and started kissing him.

They found a slow rhythm at first, her body adjusting to the feel of him inside of her. He held her, lifting her legs and exploring her as he moved in slow sure strokes. Then he started to speed up. His motions grew harder and faster, and that pressure built higher in her. She could feel the tight reins he was holding on himself as he made love to her, slowly letting go here and there to increase her pleasure.

Before long they were in a tempest of passion, and she never wanted it to stop. He lifted her a little more, changing the angle so he hit that spot deep inside of her that would not be denied. Between one thrust and the next, her pleasure spilled over, and she cried out as her body clenched down on him, spasming in the most intense orgasm she had ever had.

"Oh fuck, Naomi, I..." he tried to speak, but instead he growled and delivered one more powerful thrust into her before he was writhing and shaking as he released deep inside of her.

They lay there locked together for what felt like an eternity before he fell next to her and pulled her to him. He kissed her softly, brushing her sweaty hair away from her face.

"Naomi," he whispered again. "Are you okay?"

"Yes," she purred and then leaned in to kiss him. "I'm very okay."

"Good," he answered and smiled.

She loved how cautious he had been with her. It had been something she needed, but she hoped he didn't stay that way. She wanted him to let go as much as he had made her let go. They didn't sleep much that night. After catching their breath, Naomi took her time giving back to him. They made love in every position they could think of until the two of them collapsed in blissful exhaustion long past sunrise.

CHAPTER TWENTY-FIVE

NAOMI

She woke up in such delicious soreness that she almost didn't want to finish waking up. Her sleep had been deep and dreamless, and all she wanted was more. Her body had curled up against Damion, who had sprawled out with only a hint of the sheet crossing over him as he continued to sleep.

A smile curled her lips as she leaned up and watched him. He looked so peaceful sleeping. Oh, how she wished they could stay in their little bubble and never have to leave. In that moment, everything felt perfect. She hadn't felt that kind of serenity in far too long. For once, her chest wasn't tight, and her eyes didn't feel like they were on the verge of tears.

Taking a deep breath, she shifted until she was straddling his lap and began to kiss over his chest and up his neck. A moan echoed from his throat as he reached up and ran his fingers down her back. To think, he had never woken up with a woman in his bed before. She still couldn't believe he had lived that long and been with that many girls, yet never shared the bed before.

"Good morning," she whispered, continuing to kiss over his body. His skin was salty from sweat, and she loved that she had been the one to make him that way.

"Morning," he groaned a bit. One of his eyes cracked open and he gave her a sleepy grin. "Is this what I get for breakfast today?"

"Yes," she answered.

He chuckled and then kissed her as he lifted her and shifted their bodies. She made love to him one more time, waking him up with pleasure. And as they came back down from it, she sighed in pure contentment. She had not realized just how much she missed having the touch of someone in her life. Her body and soul had been starving for it and he had fed that craving, showing her that it was okay to let someone into her life again.

"I need food and a shower," Damion groaned, rolling them so he was next to her. They kissed and he nibbled playfully at her. She wasn't sure she had ever seen him smile the way he was in that moment, and she wanted to memorize every second of it.

"Food is overrated," Naomi protested.

"This coming from my chef. Shame on you," he teased and then pulled away to sit up on the side of the bed. "You could join me in the shower, though."

Naomi laughed as she got out of the bed. She no longer felt shy about her body. All of her insecurities had disappeared in the course of the night.

Damion started the shower and then pulled her into it with him. As much as she wanted to take advantage of him again, they both held back to actually bathe. He took his time washing her hair and running the soap over her body. "I'm going to have to get some of your stuff to keep here," he said as he used the removable shower head to rinse the soap from her body.

"You don't have to do that," she answered, even though it made her feel special.

"I know I don't have to, but I want to. I want you to feel comfortable here and have what you need," he answered. He kissed the back of her neck, and a shiver ran down her spine. She felt like she was in a fairytale and didn't want midnight to come. If they left the boundaries of his trailer, everything could go wrong, and that was the last thing she wanted to happen.

However, reality didn't work that way. No matter how much she wanted to protest leaving the room, she knew they had to get back to life. But how could she return to the real world after the night she had shared with him. Surely everyone would notice that she was a changed person.

"Naomi?" Damion asked, and she realized she had zoned out, lost in her own thoughts.

"Oh, umm, did you say something?" she asked, turning to face him.

"No, but we should get out of the shower. The water will get cold on us, and I've had enough cold showers recently," he teased and then kissed her softly.

They got out and dressed, and then it was time to leave the shelter of the trailer. Was he having as much of a dilemma with this as she was? Probably not. She had to be overthinking everything, but it was keeping other, more intrusive, thoughts at bay.

"I have a production meeting before we start night shoots tomorrow. At least we stayed up late. I'll be ready for night shoots now," he teased as he tied his shoes.

"That is one way to see it." She laughed. "Let me get you some food before you have to go. Do you want actual breakfast food?"

"Yeah, that would be good. I would usually go on a run, but I think I'm sore enough," he said. His eyes darkened and the look made her stomach clench remembering the workout they had shared the night before.

The time had come for them to leave their cocoon. With how late it was, the sun was bright and hot. She hadn't expected it. How long had they been in that room? Logically she knew, but she almost felt like one of those people who escape tunnels after years in darkness.

Damion took her hand, and they walked together over to the kitchen. Maria was outside of her trailer on the phone, and she looked over to them and shook her head.

"Maria okay?" Naomi asked, making her way toward the kitchen door.

"She isn't happy with my life choices right now, but they are mine and not hers," he answered following behind.

Usually, Damion sat out at the table while she cooked, but apparently, he wasn't ready to leave her side, either. Naomi let her mind get into work mode, pulling out ingredients and laying them on the counter. She didn't have time to make the biscuits, so he was winning the battle today, but she still had every faith she would win the war. One day, he would eat one.

"What are you making?" he asked, standing out of the way.

"Egg scramble. It has all the stuff you like and doesn't take as long. I'll also cut up some fruit," she answered as she started to chop up some of the vegetables.

"You know, I am capable of eating whole fruit," he said and then went to the fridge and pulled out an apple.

"Sure, so long as you don't cut my pay for not working as hard," she answered with a playful tone in her voice.

"We will see after your performance review," he teased back before taking a big bite out of the apple.

"Oh, look at you eating all those carbs," Naomi teased.

"Fruit carbs are different," he protested.

They broke out laughing, but she was right, regardless of his protest to the contrary. "Yes, selective carbs. That is how nutrition works."

"Well, processed food is bad, right, so there is a difference between that," Damion said as if trying to sound like he understood things.

"First, ultra processed food can be bad, but that is a completely different argument. A lot of food that we consume is processed. Last I checked, you don't go outside and cut a steak off of a cow, so your food is processed since you buy it already cut up and ready to go. So saying processed food is bad is a misnomer. Besides, by your own fucked up logic, my biscuits shouldn't offend you so badly," Naomi explained.

"I am too hungry for such a scientific conversation." Damion laughed, avoiding admitting she was right.

"Well, your food is almost ready," she answered.

She sautéed the vegetables for a bit before adding the eggs. Once everything was combined and cooked, she sprinkled on a little bit of cheese and then plated everything. They didn't bother going to the table, and instead ate leaning over the kitchen counter. It was sweet and full of joy, and completely reminded her of Paul.

CHAPTER TWENTY-SIX

DAMION

He noticed the instant the bubble broke. They had been laughing and playing, but then her face fell, and her eyes grew distant. Something had happened. A thought had entered her mind to take away the high of the night they had shared. He knew things wouldn't be perfectly seamless, but he had hoped the bliss would last a little longer. It all happened like a blink, and the world felt as if it had grown colder.

When she had woken him up making love to him, he had felt a joy that had never been in his life before. He cared about this girl. More than he thought he was ever capable of, and he knew that meant fighting the ghost in her past. It had been laid out for him from the start, but he had no idea how he was going to do it. His life had been filled with single-serving one-night stands. The way he felt for Naomi was fresh and new and terrifying. As much as he didn't want to admit it, he knew he was falling in love with her, but being in love with someone still in love with someone else was going to be torture.

Taking a deep breath, he reached out and took her hand. She turned that distant look to him and blinked a couple of times. Naomi visibly shook her head and smiled. Whatever thought had crossed her mind, she was trying to push it away.

"Hey, listen, I don't want you to be afraid to feel however you feel," he said, pulling her in closer to him. "I know this is a lot. It is for me too."

She licked her lips and nodded. "I'm sorry, just processing."

"I get it," he answered and leaned down to kiss her. To him, he was reminding her of how he felt and what was real. He had no intentions of replacing the man she had loved before, but that man wasn't there and was never coming back. Damion was alive and had every intention of staying by her side.

"So, umm, do you want me to make you a lunch for the set, or is the meeting short?" she asked, and he knew she was just trying to get her focus on something less emotional.

"Actually, how about this. The meeting should only be an hour or two. How about after the meeting I take you into town. I can take you to dinner and maybe we can go dancing or something," he suggested. "You know, give you a night off of cooking."

She blushed, and he felt his body come to life. He loved that she blushed. She was very much a woman but still had so much innocence. "Yeah, that would be fun."

"Good, then, I will leave you to this, and I'm going to head off to my meeting." He leaned down and gave her a long-heated kiss. He wasn't sure he would ever get enough of kissing her, and he never wanted to find out. "See you soon."

He had to pry himself away to leave the kitchen trailer, and he started toward the set. Maria was still in front of her trailer on the phone. He wondered what she was doing, but it was her job to deal with all of the calls, so he didn't have to.

"Okay, I got to go. Send me over the proposal," she said before hanging up the phone. "So, how fucked are you?"

"Very good and fucked," he answered and chuckled.

Maria swatted him and then shoved his shoulder a bit. Sometimes they acted like they were brother and sister, and that was how he knew she was perfect for working with him.

"You know what I mean. I don't need the details. How bad is this going to mess things up?"

"Look, Naomi working with me was always temporary. I'm sure we can get through the rest of this without any issues. Jessie will have her baby and at least the work side of things will go back to normal. I don't know what you are so bent out of shape for," Damion answered.

"You don't think big picture. If you and Naomi have a falling out, that can be the end of your career. All she would have to do is go to the press, and your whole world blows up," Maria pointed out.

"She isn't the type to do that. Allicia would but not Naomi. Besides, I don't plan for anything to go wrong," Damion answered.

"Oh, foolish boy. How I wish everyone could live in your head. No one plans for things to go wrong, but that doesn't stop it from happening. You can't plan your whole life off of the happy high of new love, and don't tell me you aren't falling in love with her. I'm not stupid. You have never let a woman stay the night with you, and now you have her over every night. You are so in love it's almost gross," Maria said. She was just calling it all out.

"I don't know what it is, but it is different for me. It's also terrifying. Naomi has a past, and I have no idea how to compete with that," he said. They were getting closer to the set, and he really didn't want to have this conversation where others could hear.

"You don't. That is all there is to it. You be the something different. There is no way to compete with the past," Maria said, stopping and turning him to look at her. Apparently, she didn't want to get too close to strangers either. "Look, you know I only want the best for you. I'm being hard on you about this because you are venturing into territory you have never been in, and I know you can be stupid sometimes, but I want the best for you. Naomi... well from what I have managed to find out, she is complicated. She has a nightmare chasing her. You can either shield her from it or you can fight it, but you can't do both. Make your choice."

Damion hadn't thought of it that way. He had a lot to think about when it came to Naomi. Unfamiliar territory was not the easiest terrain, but she was worth it. He just hoped he would be able to show her it was okay.

The conversation came to an end with those words, and the two of them made their way to the meeting. Damion had never been more desperate for a film to wrap up in his life. Usually he liked being on set, but for the first time in as long as he could remember, he was ready for a real break. He could use it to get to know Naomi and find a way to make whatever they had work.

"You look rested," Allicia said, walking up to him and hugging him. It was a distant almost cold hug. Though her face was smiling, her actions were anything but happy. She did not like that he had continued to reject her.

"Well, I got really good sleep last night. I should be good for night shoots now," he answered, kissing her cheek before they started walking together.

Maria made a huff, and Allicia gave the woman a curious look. Damion was not about to explain. "That's good. I almost prefer night shoots. Especially here. It is so hot. I mean LA is hot too, but it's different. Here you just feel like you are in a swamp all of the time."

"You sort of are in a swamp. There are actually some within the forest," Damion answered.

"Well, you get what I'm saying. I prefer it back in LA where I don't have to worry about this damn humidity," Allicia continued to complain.

"No, instead you have to worry about earthquakes and wildfires," Damion said, shaking his head.

"Rather an earthquake than any of this any day," Allicia groaned, her hand swatting at something in the air. A bug must have been flying around her face.

Damion looked back in time to see Maria making a motion like she was choking herself in response to Allicia's whining. At least they agreed on that. How Damion had ever dated the woman was beyond him.

CHAPTER TWENTY-SEVEN

NAOMI

Naomi didn't have a lot of clothing for going out on dates. She had never really gone out a lot. Her dates with Paul had always been more casual, but Damion was a fancier kind of guy, so she wanted to dress a little nicer. Up until that point, he had only seen her made up when she had interviewed for the job. After that, she had stayed pretty natural. They were in the middle of the forest, after all. It was hard enough to keep from sweating to death, much less keep makeup from melting. Naomi had no idea how they handled it on the set. Of course, they probably had better products than her drug store stuff.

"Are you really not going to tell me anything?" Jessie asked. She had called her friend to tell her that she had taken her advice and chat while she was getting ready.

"I'm not a kiss and tell kind of girl," Naomi answered.

"That is not true at all. When you kissed him, you told me all about it. Come on, was it everything you fantasized when you were lying in bed in high school?" Jessie teased. "I need some real gossip. I'm going crazy being home all the time."

Naomi sighed and picked up her phone so she could look at her friend. "It was nothing like I fantasized. It was better. So much better," Naomi answered and knew she was turning the color of a strawberry.

"Oh wow. You know, I have always heard that he was good," Jessie teased. "So now the important question. How are you holding up?"

"Better than I thought I would, but he knew when I started over-thinking," Naomi answered. Once Damion had left for his meeting she had a bit of a breakdown. She found herself sitting on the floor of the kitchen crying. Not that she was upset over being with Damion. He made her feel so cared for and alive. If she didn't know better, she would think he loved her. No, she cried over the fact that little by little her relationship with Damion was pushing out the pain of losing Paul.

"I'm proud of you. I know it isn't easy. I couldn't imagine going through what you did, but you deserve to be happy. Damion, spoiled as he is, is a good guy. I wouldn't have worked for him as long as I did if I didn't truly believe that," Jessie said.

"What if I forget all about Paul, though?" Naomi said, and she could feel tears starting to sting her eyes.

"That will never happen. I promise you that, and I don't think Damion would let that happen either. I've talked to him, and as much as he has grown to care about you, he knows how important Paul was in your life, but girl, Paul is gone," Jessie answered.

"I know, but I still think about him every day," Naomi answered. She looked up and blinked quickly trying to keep from ruining her makeup. No way was she going to succeed at fixing it.

"So do I. That is how I know you will never forget him. He wasn't even as special to me as he was to you, and I think of him every single day. Love doesn't stop at death, but life doesn't stop either. I really want you to have fun tonight, and I do want to start getting more details. If you two are going to call me all the time with your problems,

I should get paid with dirty details. It's only fair," Jessie said, changing the subject back to a more teasing tone.

"Well, you can try to get them out of him. I'm not talking," Naomi said. She laughed and stuck her tongue out at her friend. If she couldn't be there with her, at least Naomi could call her and see her face. Being away from Jessie had been difficult too.

"Don't think I won't, and Damion likes to talk to me. I'm sure I will get all the details, even the things you don't want me to know," Jessie teased before she made a distinct hiss of pain.

Naomi felt her heart stop for a second, "Are you okay?"

"Yes, I'm fine. Carrying human life is not an easy feat. I don't recommend it. The baby was just doing something, and it was not pleasant. I swear the thing pinched me," Jessie answered.

"You tried for so long to get pregnant. Now you don't recommend it?" Naomi asked, arching a brow at her friend.

"Not at all. Have the man carry it," Jessie joked. She knew Jessie was excited about the baby, but the pregnancy had not been easy with the doctor putting her on bed rest very early.

"Well, you will tell me if something happens," Naomi said, her tone serious.

"Yes, I will tell you. I can't believe how fast this is all going by. It's going to be here before we know it," Jessie said.

Naomi watched as her friend looked down at her tummy. While Naomi couldn't see Jessie's stomach, she knew Jessie was petting it. That was the bad thing about her being away. She wasn't there to go through all of this with her friend.

"Well, I should get off of here. I need to finish getting ready for my, umm, date," Naomi said. She blew a kiss to Jessie and then turned off the call.

Luckily, she had managed not to ruin her makeup. Searching through her closet, she found a summer dress. It wasn't fancy, but it was nice enough for a night out in the middle of nowhere Georgia. Hopefully Damion didn't have anywhere too fancy in mind. She certainly wouldn't have anything for that.

She had just finished putting her hair in a half up half down style when she heard a knock on her door. A huge smile spread over her face as she went to answer it. Damion was standing there waiting for her. He was dressed in black jeans and white button up shirt. It was about on par with her dress, and she was glad she wasn't underdressed.

"You look beautiful," he whispered, taking her hand and helping her out of the RV. Once her feet were on the ground, he leaned down and kissed her softly.

"Thank you. You look handsome yourself," she answered.

"So, I heard about this little cantina in town that has amazing food and dancing. I thought it would be a good place for us. I don't know how much dancing you actually do; I've only ever danced in the rain with you," he said, walking her toward a black limo. A driver held the door open for them, and they slid into the back before the driver shut the door.

"Well, I'm not a dancer, but I'm sure I can wiggle along to just about anything," she answered. Naomi loved music almost as much as food and often danced. She may not have ever studied it, but she enjoyed it all the same.

Damion gave the driver the address of where they were going, and he sped off toward town. It would take them a while to get out of the forest and into town, so Naomi listened while Damion went over his meeting and everything that happened throughout his evening.

"Oh, and Allicia is driving me insane. Any time she can, she is bringing up us getting together. I hate it."

Naomi wasn't prepared for the jealousy she felt hearing that. She wasn't sure what she and Damion were, but she certainly didn't want another woman with him if he was with her. "Are you going to tell her about us?"

"I don't know, and not because I don't want people to know. I would shout it to the world if I could. It's just, if people know we are together they will start bothering you. With how new this is, and how long it has been for you, I'd rather us take our time and work out us before throwing that complication into the mix."

Naomi honestly had not thought about what it meant to date Damion. It wasn't like he was a normal person with a normal job. Most of his life was out there for the world to see. He was constantly being pictured and followed by paparazzi. If they were dating, they would do the same to her, hoping to get her to spill some sort of juicy information. That was a lot to think about. "Should we actually be going out?"

"What? Yes! It will be fine. Most of the time, when I go out, nothing's said. Mainly because I usually go out with so many different people, but we probably won't go out consistently for a while. Keep people off the trail, you know," he answered.

His look said he was worried. Maybe he knew that bringing this up was another wrench they had yet to throw into the mess. Her issues with Paul and his with commitment were enough, but juggling the press was a whole other world that she hadn't even considered. Naomi tried to smile, but she knew it didn't reach her eyes.

"Hey, don't stress out about it. I already have security at the cantina, and with the film shooting in this area, everything is extra protected. We are going to have a good time. We can talk more about my unconventional life down the road, when we are ready," he said.

She wasn't sure if she was ever going to be ready for that kind of life. People would always be watching them, and if anything went right or wrong it would be on the front of all the gossip magazines. How would she be able to go through a grocery store line when her face was on the magazine next to her?

Chapter Twenty-Eight

Naomi

B y the time they got to the restaurant, she had calmed down from her mini panic attack. Damion was right. It was all too new for her to stress out about. They were going to go and have fun and take each day one step at a time. The time would come when they would have to discuss how them being together would work in his world, but they were not there yet.

When they pulled into the restaurant parking lot, they were greeted with the sound of music echoing out from the building. Damion took her hand, and they walked in together. He had apparently already set up for a table because they were escorted in right away. The smell of the food was intoxicating, and she could feel her stomach rumble. It had been a long time since she had gone out to eat. After all, it was her job to do the cooking. Someone came by and put a basket of chips on the table with two little cups of salsa and let them know their waiter would be by shortly.

"You get whatever you want," Damion said as he started to look over the menu.

"So, I guess that means we aren't splitting the check," Naomi teased.

"Only if you insist," Damion joked back.

The waiter came by, and Damion ordered a plate of street tacos and a beer. Naomi wasn't sure what she expected, but that combination was not it. "Umm, you do realize you just ordered a plate and glass of carbs. Right?"

"Woman, take a night off." He laughed.

Naomi burst out laughing before she turned to the waiter and made her order. She got a plate of enchiladas and a margarita. The waiter smiled, having laughed at the joke as well before leaving to put in their order. The two of them got busy eating chips, and Damion pulled his chair around to be closer to her so he could lean over and whisper naughty thoughts into her ear. Each time he did, she found herself blushing more and more.

"I love that, you know," he whispered before kissing her lightly.

"Love what?" she asked.

"That you blush like that. It makes you even more beautiful," he answered.

Naomi turned and kissed him softly. Being out with a man made her feel different, more open and free. She was happy, actually happy, and she hadn't even realized it happened. At some point since meeting Damion, she had let go of some of her pain and found a way to smile again.

Before long, their meals were delivered, and they ate. The drinks kept flowing, and they just fell into a comfortable conversation. Once the meal was done, Damion took her hand and led her out on the dance floor, where dancers of every skill level were already scattered. Some just swayed and bounced while others were fully shaking it in intricate salsas. It was beautiful and passionate, and when Damion pulled her to him, she fell right into step. No, they couldn't salsa and cha cha like the best of them, but they did what they did, and it was fun. He was a good dancer, and she loved the way he moved with her.

In their own way, they mimicked the dancers around them, getting lost in the music. It was almost as good as making love. Now and then he would kiss her before twirling her around. Song after song they danced, letting the night take them away. Now and then they would catch their breath and get a drink, but mostly they danced. Just as it had the night before, the world around them disappeared so only the two of them existed.

"Damion!" someone called out, breaking into their little bubble.

Naomi followed where Damion looked and saw Allicia coming toward them. She was dressed in a very sexy red dress that hugged every curve and plunged low to give a very appetizing view of her breasts. Her hair was styled in waves on the side of her head, and her makeup was flawless. This woman exuded beauty, and she was coming toward them to talk to her man. Was Damion even her man? They hadn't really put a label on their relationship.

"Fuck," Damion growled and turned toward Naomi. "Whatever she says, don't let her get to you. She will try."

"Damion! I didn't know you would be here. I heard about this place from a couple of people on the crew. They said it was the best place for a night out. Since I know we're going to night shoots, I thought it would be nice to get out and have a fun night before that starts," Allicia, the most perfect-looking woman in the world, said.

"Yeah, it's always nice to get away. Umm, Naomi, this is Allicia Rockford. Allicia, this is Naomi.," Damion introduced.

"Nice to meet you," Naomi said, holding her hand out.

A fake smile was plastered on Allicia's face, but she took Naomi's and gave a gentle shake. "Pleasure, I'm sure. So, Damion, why don't you save me a dance for later?"

"I can't. I'm here with someone," Damion answered. "Have fun, though. It's a nice place."

"Hey, don't be like that. I'm sure Natalie won't mind," Allicia said. "It isn't like there won't be another girl tomorrow."

"My name is Naomi, and he said no. Why don't you go find a groupie who doesn't mind kissing your ass," Naomi said, surprised at the words that came out of her mouth.

Apparently, Allicia didn't appreciate them. "Excuse me?"

"I said..." Naomi started moving toward the tall beauty. "Go find someone else to dance with. Damion is busy."

"You aren't seriously going to let her talk to me like that. Are you Damion?" Allicia said, dismissing Naomi all together.

"Yes, I am. I'm here with her, and no, there won't be another woman tomorrow." Damion stopped for a second. He told Naomi earlier that he wasn't ready to tell anyone about them because of the implications it would have to her life. However, she could tell he was fighting with that. "Naomi and I are..."

"You are what?" Allicia sneered.

"We're together and have been for a while. Now leave us alone," Naomi said, pulling Damion back.

Allicia stood there shocked for a few seconds, looking back and forth between the two of them. "You can't be serious. Damion?"

"I'm very serious. Probably for the first time in my life. So I'll get back to my date now. I'll see you tomorrow on set," he answered as he pulled Naomi off of the floor and back to their table. He sat down with her next to him, not sure what to say.

"I'm sorry," Naomi whispered, brushing his hair back from his face.

"You don't have anything to be sorry for. I just don't want her messing things up for us. She is jealous and thinks she will always get her way. Maybe she would have if I hadn't met you. It wouldn't have lasted, but I may have been more welcoming to the idea. She's just pissed that she isn't getting what she wants," Damion said.

The waiter came with another round of drinks, and he gulped down half of his beer before setting the glass back down.

"Don't let her ruin our night. We already have enough issues between us to let some spoiled princess get in the mix too. She will move on," Naomi said, leaning in and kissing him.

The kiss seemed to distract him from his thoughts, and he delved into it with all he had. The intimacy stole her breath and made her hungry for something that wasn't food. "Do you want to get out of here?" Damion asked.

With Allicia there, leaving did sound like the better option. Giving him a smile, she nodded and kissed him softly again. The limo was still waiting for them when they got out of the restaurant. Damion held the door for her and then got in after her. They made sure the little barrier was up so the driver couldn't see them, and then he kissed her hard and deep.

Naomi wasn't sure if it was the confrontation with Allicia or all the alcohol, but Damion was more heated and aggressive as he devoured her kisses. He reached over and pulled her onto his lap, his hands pulling her dress higher and higher until he was able to pull it off her body. With the light color of the dress, she had been wearing white under it. His eyes roamed over her body before he started kissing her again.

She liked this side of Damion, even if it was because he was upset. He was dominant and powerful. His kisses stung in just the right way. The sweetness of the night before was gone, and Naomi wanted to feel the darker side of him. She reached down and started pulling at his belt. Damion worked on the buttons of his shirt, pulling it off as soon as he had enough of the buttons undone to toss it away.

He lifted his hips to pull his pants down just enough to free himself and then reached up with one hand to unsnap her bra and toss it away. He kissed her hard, almost painfully, and it made her cry out in his mouth. They didn't talk. There was no air for talking. The energy between them sizzled as she rolled her hips against his hardness, only the thin cotton of her panties separating them.

He seemed to know her thoughts as well. He lifted her and pulled her panties to the side before impaling her on him. They both cried out as Naomi began to bounce and roll on top of him. He gripped the back of her neck and held her to him. The kissing had stopped, making way for the sounds of their pleasure as Naomi rode him hard and fast, a complete contrast to the night they had shared before. This was raw and fierce... carnal.

Damion guided her and thrust to meet her, his grip nearly bruising. She could hear him groaning and chanting "fuck" over and over as she did just that. This wasn't the sharing of love; this was the savage release of unbridled need. They didn't hold back. They didn't wait for it to be perfect. They let it happen, and when the flood of pleasure rolled through her and she lost her rhythm, he gripped her and took control. She screamed out over and over as he slammed himself up into her until he joined her, roaring out as he shook and writhed below her.

He crashed his lips to hers as they started to come down from their orgasm, and he held her to him, his grip loosening a bit to trail soft pets up and down her spine. His touch made her shiver, and something about it made him moan.

"I will never get enough of you," he moaned against her lips and then kissed her hard and deep, his body already hardening for her again. The night was only getting started, and no room was left for soft and gentle.

Chapter Twenty-Nine

Damion

Night shoots were not going well. Allicia was pissed, and she had no problem letting everyone know. Thankfully she didn't tell everyone about Naomi, but she did make everyone well aware of the fact that she was angry with Damion over something. Filming a romance when the two stars were at odds with each other was never an easy process, and everything had slowed down because of it.

"I don't know what has gotten into the two of you, but two weeks ago you were giving me the best performances of your career and now nothing. Fix it! Whatever it is, fix it!" the director said, walking over to where they were.

They were supposed to be shooting a scene where the two of them got caught up in their passion and ended up making love against a tree. Such a simple thing that normally wouldn't have caused any problems. Even when he and Allicia broke up, they had been able to work together. As much as Damion wanted to blame it all on her, he knew it was also him. He didn't want to kiss her or touch her. Not after how she treated Naomi.

"Really, Damion? You are going to tank both of our careers over some fling that got under your skin. You are better than this," Allicia spat at him.

Damion groaned and ran his fingers through his hair. No, he didn't want to tank their careers. He needed to shake off this feeling that he was betraying Naomi by doing his job. She was well aware of what he did and hadn't said one word about it. So why was he so hung up on it? "Give me a minute."

He walked over to the catering table and grabbed a bottle of water. Taking a couple of deep breaths, he let his nerves calm before turning back. Two weeks ago, when they were supposedly doing the job of their lives, he had been thinking about Naomi every time he kissed Allicia. That had been before he actually kissed Naomi. Now he knew exactly what it would feel like. She could be his inspiration again.

Damion smiled remembering how she asked him about acting like you were in love when you had never been in love. Somehow, he understood her question. It was so much more intense than any love scene he had filmed. "Alright, I'm ready."

"Finally!" Allicia groaned.

Hair and makeup came over and started to do touch ups when a loud clap of thunder boomed out into the night. Everyone turned toward the director to see what he wanted to do. "If it rains, it rains. We are getting this shot tonight, wet or dry."

Damion walked over to Allicia and took her hand, pulling her close to him. "Look, can we just let go of what happened at the restaurant the other night. You are better than this too. Let's just move on and do what we do best."

Allicia took a deep breath and turned to look at him. For a second, he thought she was going to protest, but she didn't. Instead, she smiled and kissed his cheek. "Yeah, that would probably be best. I'm sorry I have been being such a bitch. I don't know what has gotten into me lately."

"It's fine. Now let's go to work," Damion answered.

They got into position, and he took a few deep breaths. There weren't a lot of lines in this scene. They had already filmed most of the speaking parts. They were having issues with the sex part. The director called action, and the cameras began to roll.

Damion took several steps forward and pulled Allicia to him, wrapping his arm around her and gazing down into her eyes. "I'm not sure I can wait," he whispered loudly enough to be heard by the cameras.

Wasting no time, he started kissing her, but his mind thought about that first time he kissed Naomi. Another boom of thunder echoed, which only added to the scene. Damion reached down and picked Allicia up, slamming her into a nearby tree. Her legs wrapped around him, and he thought of how good it felt when Naomi wrapped herself around him.

Rain began to pour down, and it drove him forward. They kissed hot and hard, passionately. The rain mixed with their movements and fueled the scene.

"Take me," Allicia moaned, arching back against him.

They pulled at their clothes, stripping off the appropriate amounts to make it look believable. It was all smoke and mirrors, but they still had to sell it. He rolled his body against hers, his kisses moving from her mouth. Her breath was heavy, and her hands held on to him. He fell into his work, and he was no longer letting his personal life get in the way.

They said their lines between kisses, and he gave his all to the scene. Maybe all he needed was for Allicia to apologize. They had been so at odds that it was difficult to look at her without hating her. The friction would be good for the papers but not getting a movie made.

"Cut!" the director called out, and Damion pulled away, helping Allicia to her feet. Almost instantly the passion was gone. "Yes! That was much better. I want to do another take and change the angle a bit. Damion, make sure you push the dress all the way up her hip. I want to see the long line of her leg. Oh, the rain is making this better. I hope it keeps up."

Damion laughed and shook his hair out like a dog. Allicia swatted at him, and the two of them laughed. At least the rain cooled everything off. Everyone got back into position as the camera moved locations, and they did the scene again. All told, they shot the scene four times before the director felt he got everything he needed. Lucky for them, the rain held out. By the time he was walking off set, he was ready to get dry. Even Maria had run for cover, and she almost always stayed with him on set.

"Hey, good job out there," Allicia said, coming up behind him. "You're really good at that when you want to be."

"Yeah, you too," he said and watched as she went off with a couple of the girls.

With the weight lifted, he made his way toward his trailer. He had almost gotten to it when he saw Naomi. She was standing out in the rain looking up at the sky. He stood there watching her. Something about how she was moving and the slump back of her shoulders told him she was upset. He wasn't sure what from, and he had no idea if he should go check on her or give her privacy. She had walked past their trailers near the edge of the woods as if she wanted to be alone.

Not knowing what to do, he just stood there and watched her. She was beautiful, even in her pain. The rain made her clothes cling to her and her hair hung long down her back. His heart throbbed and he wasn't sure if it was pain or some other emotion he was far less familiar with. Either way, he couldn't take his eyes off of her.

Then she turned and saw him. She raced toward him and wrapped her arms around him. She was shaking and sobbing but didn't tell him why. He didn't ask. If she wanted him to know, she would tell him. Instead, he breathed in the scent of her hair and held her until her body stopped shaking.

CHAPTER THIRTY

NAOMI

It had been weeks since Naomi had a nightmare, but the night shoots had screwed up their whole schedule. She had gotten used to sleeping again, which made everything more difficult to fight when she was alone. The shoots seemed to take longer and longer than she expected, and sometimes she was alone until long past sunrise. The night was much more difficult to deal with on her own. Damion had spoiled her.

Damion had sent her a text telling her that things were increasingly difficult on set since their altercation with Allicia. She kept telling him to try and work past it for the sake of his job. The last thing she wanted was for her relationship with him to cause problems for him at work.

It was going to be another late night, so she went into her RV and lay down with her Kindle to read more of her book. She had managed to get through a good portion of it over the last several days and had gotten into it. The night before she had been in the middle of a really good scene when Damion got back from the set, and she made him wait for her to finish before she would come over. He had laughed but had gone to shower while she finished. It was such a mundane thing.

Everything between them felt so natural, and it was terrifying to her. He seemed so comfortable with her, as if they had been together for a long time. Most of the time she felt the same until she thought about Paul. Damion seemed to know when that happened. He wouldn't say anything, but he always let her have her time. It wasn't fair to him to have to comfort her over the past, but in a way that was how their whole relationship had gotten started.

Thunder erupted, and she knew another storm was coming. They had been getting rain showers almost every day, and they made everything soggy and humid. No one was enjoying it, but that was part of the summer in Georgia. Rain was an everyday occurrence usually after a really hot tormenting day. For the most part, the rain came and went before shooting started. It sounded like that wasn't going to be the case. Maybe they would shut down filming early.

When the rain started, the steady beat of it against the window by her bed lulled her into exhaustion. Even her enjoyment of the book couldn't keep her awake, and she slowly drifted off to sleep.

She was awakened by the sound of laugher. Slowly her eyes opened, and she saw the door to her old bedroom in the house she bought with Paul. Part of her knew it was a dream, but another part had no idea. She threw the covers off her and got up, wrapping a robe around herself to pad down the hall. Jessie and Brad were in the kitchen with someone. The third person was shadowy and didn't have any true shape or features.

Thinking it was because she was still trying to wake up, Naomi walked further into the room, rubbing her eyes, but the form never solidified. Who was it? Why did it feel familiar and foreign all at once?

"Isn't he the best?" Jessie said, sliding a cup of coffee toward her.

"What?" Naomi asked, confused.

"You are so lucky," Jessie said, but nothing made sense. At some point Brad had completely disappeared.

Then everything got dark. The darkness grew thicker and thicker until the features of the house were gone, and all that remained was her and the shadowy figure. Naomi's heart started to pound hard enough that it ached and made it difficult to breathe. The shadow rushed forward and knocked her down. She frantically looked around, trying to make sense of what was happening.

Clicking of footsteps echoed through the darkness. Shadows gave way to a hazy form. It became clearer the more it entered the light until she could see Paul standing over her. He squatted down so he could look into her eyes. "You are forgetting me."

"No, I would never forget you," she said, her voice trembling with a mix of fear and sadness.

"You are forgetting me and replacing me with that... well he certainly isn't worthy of you." Paul sneered, spitting on the ground next to him.

"No, Paul, you don't understand. I love you. I will never forget you, but you're gone. Paul, you're gone," Naomi cried.

"Oh, sweet Naomi, you have him replacing me in every way. He kisses you like I did. He fucks you like you want me to. You even dance with him in the rain. That was our thing. That belonged to me!" Paul lunged forward, knocking her back.

If she had the ability to think logically, she would have known it was all a nightmare. The real Paul would never talk to her like that. He was gentle and sweet, and he loved her with all he had. This apparition wasn't speaking for him. her own fear was coming out of his mouth. The problem was she couldn't think logically. In the depths of the nightmare, the world was real. Paul was real. He pulled her to him and wrapped his arms around her.

"Feel me, Naomi."

He held her tightly to him, his arms like steel bands around her. They grew colder and colder with every passing second, but he continued to berate her about forgetting him, replacing him. She couldn't escape. The darkness encroached even more, leaving nothing but oblivion surrounding the two of them as she desperately tried to escape. The harder she pushed, the tighter his arms grew until she felt like she was completely wrapped in ice.

Naomi woke screaming and shaking. Tears were already flowing like rivers down her face. Outside the rain continued to rage on. She had no idea how long she had been asleep. Honestly, she wasn't even sure she was awake. It didn't matter. She threw the covers off and raced out of the RV.

Her head flung left and right, and she screamed into the night for Paul. The dream still lingered on her, a bruising sensation continued to pulse on her arms, and no amount of fighting it made it go away. She ran down what was left of the road until she found herself at the edge of the forest. Flinging her arms back, she looked up at the sky and tried to ground herself again.

"I haven't forgotten you. I swear, I will never forget you," she cried, the sobs painfully vibrating through her body.

She didn't hear it, only felt it. One moment, the remnants of the dream lingered and the next she could feel someone watching her. Slowly she turned and saw Damion standing there in the rain staring at her. His face was serious but his eyes soft. Without a moment of hesitation, she ran toward him and wrapped herself around him. His body was warm and real, and she needed that to sink in and take away the pain the nightmare had inflicted on her.

He gently wrapped his arms around her and rested his head on top of hers. She could hear the pounding of his heart and smell the scent of his soap along with a hint of Allicia's perfume. After a few moments of just holding her, he moved and kissed the top of her head. He didn't ask her what was wrong or push her to talk to him. He just held her and let her cry until all of the tears were gone.

Eventually the nightmare faded, and she once again felt safe, but she still had a lingering thought. Her own fear was conjuring up nightmares to remind her why she had stayed alone for so long. No matter how much Jessie told her that she would never forget Paul, and no matter how much Damion showed that he wasn't going to push that part of her away, her fear was still very much alive. She wasn't sure she could live her life without Paul in it. Even if all she had was the memory of him.

Damion must have realized that she was out of her panic, so he pulled back enough to give her a soft kiss. "Do you want to go inside?"

"I don't know," she answered.

"We don't have to. I'm already wet," he answered and gave her the slightest smile. He was trying to break the tension, and she loved that about him. Whenever she was sad or afraid, he found a way to make her smile.

"I hadn't noticed," Naomi said, but her voice was weak, and the joke did not resonate as strongly as it would have had she been able to let the sarcasm sink into the tone. Damion laughed anyway.

Slowly he started to sway with her. Dancing. *You even dance with him in the rain. That was our thing.* She heard Paul's voice whisper through her mind, and she pulled away. Damion didn't pull her back in. He let her step back and watched her. His face looked cautious and a bit confused. Naomi knew this was outside of his element. She was sure he had no idea what to do with her, and he shouldn't have to question his every move.

They stood there looking at each other for several seconds before Damion spoke. "I don't know what you want me to do. I'm trying, but I don't know."

"I'm sorry," was the only answer she had.

"You don't have to be sorry. Just tell me what you want me to do. Help me here," he said, taking a step toward her.

She stepped back again almost out of impulse. "You deserve better, Damion. You deserve someone not so broken."

"Naomi, what are you talking about?" he asked, taking another step forward.

When she went to back away, he reached out with his long arms and took her hand, pulling her closer to him. He didn't hug her or try to trap her, just didn't let her widen the distance.

"You are such a good guy, and I'm a fucking mess. You should be with someone that isn't so traumatized. I can't do this," Naomi said, and her tears came back, harder than before.

"You aren't broken or whatever you think is wrong. Naomi, please. I don't want anyone else," he said, this time pulling her close enough to him that their bodies were touching.

"That's just it, Damion. You don't want me either. I can't. I can't do this," Naomi said, breaking away and turning to go back to her RV.

"Naomi wait!" he called after her. "Naomi! I love you!"

She had gotten her hand on the handle of her door when those words burst out into the night between them. Her body froze in place, hearing him say them. How much had it cost him to actually say those words out loud. They had been playful and passionate, showing they cared for one another for weeks, but neither of them had said those three precious words.

Damion reached her and turned her to look at him. He stroked her cheek and brushed her hair away from her face. They were both dripping wet and shaking. For the first time, she realized he was trembling as hard as she was. "Naomi, I love you. You are my one. My first. Please, don't run from this."

"Damion," she whispered, but the rest of the words got stuck in her throat.

"It's okay. Don't feel pressured or anything, just don't leave," he whispered and leaned down to kiss her.

For a moment, she let him kiss her, and then she sank her fingers into his hair and started kissing him back. Their passion rose, and he picked her up, flung open the door, and carried her back to her bedroom. They kissed and touched, but there was almost a painful finality to it. He seemed to be struggling to hold on, and she almost felt like she was letting go.

CHAPTER THIRTY-ONE

NAOMI

There was a reason they always stayed over at Damion's trailer. Her RV was small. When she had gotten it, she had only intended for her to be inside. At one point she thought about getting a dog but realized that was too much responsibility for her. Waking up with Damion in her bed, she realized just how small her bedroom was. They were both still fully dressed, their clothes having dried at some point while they slept. His legs were dangling off of the bed, almost touching the wall. Of course, he was really tall, but it was still a bit funny.

If only she had it in her to be amused. Sliding out from the bed, she shuffled into her little kitchen area and put on some coffee. The day had passed on and it was already afternoon. Damion would need to get to work soon, which meant she had to get his meals ready. Naomi tried to focus on work instead of the nightmare from the night before. She felt like her heart was breaking all over again, and it made everything heavy and difficult to accomplish.

The RV shifted, and Damion came out from the back. His eyes were still partly closed, and he was holding on to the edge of the counter for stability. "I think my feet fell asleep. They are all numb."

"That's because you don't fit in my bed," she answered, and strangely the words held more meaning to her than she had expected.

"Hey, about last night," Damion started to say, turning her to look at him. He brushed his thumb along her cheek and smiled a bit. "I meant what I said. I love you. Please know that I understood from the start what I was getting into. Whatever happened last night, we can get through it."

Naomi didn't know what to say. She wasn't sure she believed that, but of course she didn't say it. "I started some coffee, but I should probably get to the kitchen and start cooking. I know you have to get to work."

Damion took in a deep breath like he was going to say something but didn't. He leaned down and kissed the top of her head before moving past her to leave. Her heart ached, heavy and deep, in a way she hadn't expected it to feel again. It had taken her so long to stop feeling so much pain after Paul died. Being with Damion was just stirring up all of those damaged memories again. Taking a deep breath, she poured herself a cup of coffee and then went to the kitchen trailer to start on the day's meals.

She got so caught up in what she was doing, she didn't realize that Damion didn't come by to get his breakfast. By that time, she knew he was already on set. He hadn't even come by to tell her he was leaving. Packing up his meal, she decided she would take it to him on set. The walk would do her some good, and she hadn't really watched him work much. Maybe watching him in his element would help her shake the lingering despair she felt.

The day was cooler, even with the sun still out. It was starting to settle below the horizon as it set. They were not far from the darkness of the night. She still hadn't gotten used to the backward schedule of the night shoots. Turning the corner, she could hear the hustle and bustle of an active set. People were rushing around, doing their jobs and ignoring her. When she got to the set, the first person she saw was Maria.

"Hey, you don't usually come out here," Maria said, giving her a side hug. "You getting a little bored being over there by yourself all night?"

"Maybe a little, but mostly I was bringing Damion some food. He didn't eat before he headed over," she answered. There was a full table of food from catering, but one look let her know it was not Damion's normal diet.

"Well, he will be happy for that then. Things seem to be going better today. Things were a bit rocky when we started working nights, but it snapped into place last night," Maria explained. "I'm sure Damion told you all about it, though, so I won't bore you with the details. You didn't happen to bring me some too. Did you?"

"Of course I did," Naomi answered and handed the bag over to Maria.

"You can get closer if you want so you can watch. They will tell you if you get too close, but so long as you don't go past the hard cam, you should be fine," Maria explained, pointing her in the direction of where the actual filming was taking place.

Damion and Allicia were acting out a scene, though Naomi had no idea what it was about. It would have probably made more sense if she had seen the whole thing or read the script. Since she had done neither, she just watched from where they were. Damion looked amazing. He moved around the set in perfect motion. Allicia moved with him as if they knew exactly where to step and what to do. They were talking about hiding from her parents or some such. Naomi wasn't really listening. Instead, she just watched how they acted together.

She remembered asking Damion once how he was able to make things look so real. He told her he just pretended to be in love, and it seemed to work. Watching the two of them together, it was hard for her to believe it was just pretend. Everything looked so real, so perfect, as if they were made for each other. Was that how it looked when he was with her?

Insecurity began to rear its ugly head, and she took a step back. Then the two of them started to kiss. At first, she thought she was going to run, but instead, she became mesmerized by the sight of them kissing as if their life depended on it. Damion had kissed her like that. Deep, hard, and full of passion.

Allicia broke the kiss and pulled away from him as if to run off, but he pulled her back to him and kissed her again, lifting her in his arms before letting her slide down his body. The whole scene was beautiful and magical. A true Hollywood illusion, but if that were the case, why did it feel so real.

Naomi turned and weaved her way out of the filming area. She saw Maria watching her, and she gave her a weak smile.

"Naomi," Maria said, holding her hand out and taking Naomi's. "It's just pretend. Don't let it fool you. They are just very good at their jobs. That's why they are still working."

"I know. I'm not upset. It's just been a hard few days. I haven't been sleeping well again," she answered.

"Nights are always difficult. It's the same for everyone, but it's all part of the job. You'll get used to it," Maria explained.

Naomi gave her another weak smile and headed back toward her RV. She could feel Maria watching her, but she didn't turn back. Was she just coming up with excuses to run? Maybe she was just letting her own fears keep her from being happy. Letting someone into her life after so long alone was no easy feat, but it had all felt too easy. Had she just decided there should be more difficulty to it, or was it just a fantasy that would never last? Naomi wasn't sure, and she knew she wasn't going to get the answer by sitting around and waiting for it to come to her.

Getting back to her RV, she went in and wrote a note for Damion, letting him know she needed to go on a drive and would be back later. She needed to clear her head, and sitting around waiting on him was not going to help.

CHAPTER THIRTY-TWO

DAMION

Maria had told Damion that Naomi came to set but left before he had a chance to see her. She had delivered his food, which he appreciated since he had been so upset that he left without eating. He wasn't upset with her. Naomi was struggling with accepting him in her life after what happened with Paul. He was well aware of that and tried not to let it bother him. No, he was just upset in general.

For the first time in his life, he had told a woman he loved her. He had always imagined it to be some magical moment where everything fell perfectly in place and they would make love for the rest of the night, just like in the movies he made. His experience had been far from it. Naomi had been crying, and he had been fighting to bring her back from whatever darkness had captured her while she was working. While the moment had been intense, it had not been so in the way he expected.

All he could hope for was that she had calmed down as the night went on. At least things had gotten better at work. After his talk with Allicia and her apology, everything had gotten back to normal. At the end of the day, they both wanted the same thing, for the movie to be a success. Nothing could happen between them that would prevent them from letting that happen.

Getting back to his trailer, he had almost expected to find Naomi waiting for him. He desperately wanted to talk to her, but instead all he found was a note:

Damion,

I need to clear my head. Everything is just happening so fast, and I'm just not sure I'm ready for it. You have done so much for me, and I could never express how much it means to me, but I'm still in a very dark place. You shouldn't have to fight my ghost. I'm just going on a drive and will be back later. Hopefully some time to myself and away from it all will give me some clarity.

Naomi,

p.s. You looked beautiful on the set today. It was like magic watching you work.

Panic started to set in. She was pulling away. It wasn't even a little at a time. No, she was pulling away in leaps and bounds. If he didn't do something, she would jump out of his reach, and he wasn't sure he was willing to let her go like that. Pulling out his phone, he called her number. It went straight to voicemail.

"Naomi, I'm done with work for the day. Look, I don't know what happened last night, but you have to know you can talk to me about it. Don't feel guilty about your ghost or whatever it is. I just want to be with you," he said, not sure if she would get the message.

When Naomi didn't call him back, he went to dial Jessie, but it was four in the morning. He had a feeling she would not appreciate being woken up over his relationship drama. Not sure what else to do, he took a shower to get any lingering scent of Allicia off of him. There was still no response when he got out. His panic growing, he threw on his workout clothes and decided to go for a run. He was exhausted but too stressed to sleep. Making sure his phone was connected to his ear buds, he took off running.

In a way he was doing the same thing Naomi had said she was doing. He ran to clear his head, but it wasn't working. It just made his mind race with more questions. He loved her. He told her he loved her. That hadn't been easy for him, and now she was gone. She had said she would be back, and of course she had to come back. She had left her RV, but that was rational thinking, and he wasn't thinking rationally.

Damion ran until his legs started to get weak, and then he ran some more until he made it back to his trailer. Naomi was sitting outside of her RV looking around as if searching for something. When she saw him, she smiled, and all the weight he felt heavily on his soul lifted. He ran over to her and squatted down so he could look in her eyes.

"Hey," he whispered, wanting to give her the opportunity to speak first.

"Hey, sorry I wasn't here when you got back," she said, reaching over and brushing his hair from his eyes.

"That's okay. Do you feel better?" he asked, loving the feel of her fingers on him.

"Honestly, no, I don't. I'm not okay right now, Damion," she answered, and he looked down, trying not to show how much that hurt him. He needed to be stronger for her.

"What can I do?" he asked, moving in closer. He fell to his knees so he could wrap his arms around her from where she was sitting.

"I don't know. I wish I did, but I don't," she answered, leaning down and kissing the top of his head.

That had to be a good sign. She wasn't pushing him away. "What happened last night? Everything has been going so well, but then last night something changed. What was it?" Damion asked, looking up and cupping her cheek in his hand. Never in his life had he ever felt so powerless and lost. This woman had turned his world upside down.

"It's more complicated than that. Damion, I didn't come here to fall in love. I came here to work," she said.

"Same with me. We don't always have control of that, though. Trust me. This isn't something I am taking lightly. You know I have never felt this for anyone. You are my one. Don't you see that?" he pleaded, taking her hand in his and kissing it.

She smiled, and just that small gesture filled his whole body with the fire of hope. "Infinity and one," she whispered, and he knew she remembered their conversation from that first drunken night.

"Yeah, infinity where it doesn't count. One where it matters most," he whispered and leaned up to lightly kiss her lips.

His soul begged for her to tell him she felt the same. It felt like he had a knife stabbed into his gut, and if only she would answer it would sew up the pain.

"All of it matters," she said against his lips. "At least, it does for me." She kissed him back. What did all of this mean? He knew he should stop and get answers, but he was too afraid to. Kissing felt good, touching felt good.

She moved onto the ground with him, and their kisses grew more feral. The sun was rising, and the warmth of it was nothing compared to the heat growing between the two of them. When she kissed him, nothing in the world mattered. When she touched him, the universe was still.

They were exposed to the world. Anyone could walk by and see them making out in front of her RV, but neither of them seemed to care. He let her lead the kiss in whatever direction she was comfortable. When she pulled off his shirt, he let her, wanting her to do whatever would make her feel better. He was taking his lead from her. She broke the kiss and led those sweet lips down his neck, not seeming to care that he was sweaty from running.

Damion didn't take any kind of control until things started to get to a point that they actually needed the privacy. While he wasn't a fan of the size of her RV, it was the closest refuge they had. Wrapping his arms around her, he picked her up and carried her inside, setting her down on the kitchen counter. Safely out of view, he let her take control once more.

She pulled off her own shirt before reaching to him and sliding his shorts down. Her nails raked down his back, and he arched into the painful sting as it sent a wave of pleasure over him.

Lifting her just a bit, he got her pants and panties off, and then she hooked her leg around his waist and pulled him in closer to her. His height gave him the advantage of being better on level with her. He shifted them just a bit and then thrust into her body. She cried out the moment he did, and a wave of electricity shot through every nerve of his body.

Everything got primal from there. They kissed and bit at each other as he savagely pounded his body into her. Her legs pulled at him, guiding him to move harder and faster. Part of him knew it had to be painful, but at the same time, it all felt so savagely blissful that he didn't dare stop or question it.

They became a twisted being of pain and pleasure and everything in between. Her nails, his teeth, her cries, his screams. It was dark and delicious all at once, and when he released into her, he was blinded by the intensity of it. They both screamed out into the abyss that had been surrounding them.

For a moment he didn't think he could move. He collapsed into her, barely able to hold himself up. The room was filled only with the sound of their heavy breaths and pounding hearts. In the back of his mind a nagging fear told him not to say anything. If he spoke, if she spoke, it would ruin everything. So, he didn't. He instead kissed her and touched her and showed her with his body just how desperately he needed her in his life.

CHAPTER THIRTY-THREE

NAOMI

Neither of them had said anything in what felt like hours. They had made love to the point they both collapsed to the floor of her RV. Any time either of them opened their mouth to speak the other stopped them with kisses that lead to sex. Hours had gone by, and they were both sweaty and aching... exhausted.

She now sat with her back against the refrigerator and her legs crossed at the ankle in front of her. Damion was sitting across from her leaning against the cabinet by the sink. He had one knee up and his other leg bent beneath it. He was too tall to extend his legs forward. They had been sitting there for a while, not speaking and not looking at each other. The tension in the air between them made the air thick and difficult to breathe. One of them needed to say something.

Neither of them did.

She felt him turn to look at her, and she turned away, feeling the sting of tears start to form in her eyes. Her drive hadn't helped. If anything, it had made it worse. He had told her he loved her, and she had run. She was still running.

"Naomi," he whispered.

Every instinct in her told her to reach out and kiss him, make the conversation stop, but they were too exhausted to go on. Everything hurt, but mostly it was her heart. He had told her he loved her, and she hadn't been brave enough to tell him she felt the same. She hadn't been brave enough to admit it to herself, but it was there, burning inside of her and making everything in her life more complicated.

"Say something," he said, his voice still quiet. There was no conviction behind his words. He didn't actually want her to say something because he knew what she knew. Anything she said was going to hurt.

Taking a deep breath, she looked up at the ceiling because it was easier than looking at him. "I have to go."

Those words shattered her. If she really needed to leave, why did it hurt so bad? She was running. She was afraid, and she was running. Deep down, she knew that was the truth, but she wasn't stopping herself.

"Don't," Damion whispered, his voice cracking at the end.

"I have to," she said.

"Why?" he asked.

"Damion," she whispered, finally turning to look at him.

The look in his eyes shot daggers through her soul, and the tears she had been fighting started to fall down her cheeks.

"No, tell me why you have to leave," he said, shifting to move closer to her.

She didn't want him to move closer. If he moved closer to her, they would fall back into the cycle of making love and not talking. They were putting off the inevitable.

"I have to," she said. Even in that moment she couldn't let the words past her lips. They hung deep in her throat, choking her. *I love you*. It seemed like the simplest thing in the world to say, yet it scraped her insides like she had swallowed broken glass.

"That isn't a reason, Naomi. What happened that makes you want to run now? Give me something real. If you're going to leave me, at least give me a reason for it," he said, pushing up from the floor.

She could see that anger was taking the place of his pain. He searched around them to find his clothes. His body was tense and shaking, and part of her was screaming to make it go away. To comfort him from the pain she was causing him, but the part pushing her away was stronger.

"Damion, what do you want me to say?" she cried. She couldn't stand. Her legs felt like they were made of lead, and if she tried to push up, she would just topple over.

"I don't know, but something other than you are just leaving. Tell me you love me, and it hurts too much. Tell me you hate me, and you don't want to see me again. Tell me something, but don't just tell me you have to leave without a damn reason behind it. I gave myself to you. I opened up to you. You can at least give me a fucking reason why you have to go," he said, his fist pounding down on the counter. A cabinet popped open, and silverware rattled under the weight of his attack. "Just say something."

When she didn't answer, he shook his head and threw his shorts on before storming out of the RV. Outside she heard him roar out the word "fuck," and the tension in her broke. She didn't just cry. It was more than that. It was full body wails of pain. What was wrong with her? She had a man willing to accept her, flaws and all, and she was running from him. She curled in on herself, taking a fetal position as she shook and cried. Damion didn't come back. He was gone, and she had been the one to push him out.

"What am I supposed to do?" she sobbed finding her shirt and wiping her face free of tears and snot.

Finally pushing past her pain and finding her breath, she managed to sit up. She crawled into her bedroom and got dressed. When she went to unhook her RV, Damion wasn't there. She couldn't hear anything from his trailer, and part of her wanted to go and see him. She was making a mistake. She knew it deep in her soul, but when she tried to make it right, she froze.

Once everything was packed up and inside, she started up the RV and drove away. She had to get away. She had to think. The relationship with Damion had grown too fast for her and she wasn't able to process it all. Her phone rang and she saw it was Jessie. Had Damion called her to talk some sense into her? Probably.

Ignoring the call, she just drove.

CHAPTER THIRTY-FOUR

DAMION

Glass shattered, furniture broken all around him, Damion wasn't sure he had ever felt so angry in his entire life. She left. Naomi had actually packed up her RV and left. He had stood there at the window watching her, the voice inside his head screaming at him to stop her, but he couldn't. If she really thought she needed to leave, he wasn't going to stop her. The moment her RV had disappeared from sight, he called Jessie. At least it was no longer so early that it was rude to call.

"Hey, what's up," she said answering the call. She sounded tired but still happy to hear from him. Naomi must not have talked to her yet.

"She left," he said, feeling another piece of his heart break off.

"What do you mean she left?" Jessie asked, her voice becoming more focused, concerned.

"I mean exactly what I said. Naomi packed up and left," he answered.

"What the hell happened? I thought everything was going good," Jessie said, and he could hear the worry in her voice.

"That's just it, I have no idea why she left. We were fine. Then a couple of days ago I came back from set, and she was freaking out. She was scared and upset, and my fucking dumb ass chose that moment to tell her I loved her like that was going to make any difference," he said, collapsing against the wall and sliding down. Everything in his trailer was broken or in shambles. The floor was the only place for him to sit.

"Damion, oh god. Let me try to call her. Let me see if I can find out what's going on. She hasn't said anything to me about being upset. I had no idea," Jessie said.

"Don't. It will only make things worse," Damion whispered and hung up. He didn't want Jessie to feel sorry for him. He had done this to himself. Crawling over to his fridge, he flung it open and took out the bottle of vodka he had bought for Naomi.

They hadn't drunk much of it, but he was about to fix that. He didn't take it shot by shot. He gulped it down until he could no longer feel the burn. He drank it like it water and then grabbed whatever bottle was in there next. He drank until he could no longer feel the pain, where the alcohol took over and he collapsed into darkness.

His eyes were heavy, and he couldn't get them to fully open, but someone was screaming at him. "Naomi?" he asked into the room. Had she come back?

"No. Damion, what the fuck is going on?" a woman's voice demanded. It wasn't Naomi, so it didn't matter.

"Leave me alone," he groaned and closed his eyes again. He curled his body trying to find warmth. It was freezing, and he could barely breathe.

Whoever it was in his room grabbed a fist full of his hair and pulled him up by it. "I'm not leaving you until I know what the fuck is happening. Your place is trashed, Naomi is gone, and you smell like a distillery and sex. So again, what the fuck happened?"

The voice was Maria's. It had taken him that long to realize it, but he was finally able to focus enough to hear it. He reached out to pat her cheek but missed and fell back over. Apparently, he hadn't slept off enough of the alcohol. His stomach was twisted, and he was sure if he moved any more, he was going to throw up.

"She left," he said and pulled his knees to his chest.

"Why did she leave?" Maria asked, trying to get answers.

"I love her," he said as if that would make it all make sense.

"Snap out of it, Damion," Maria said, smacking at his cheek.

"Stop it! I'm going to puke!" he screamed.

He tried to crawl toward the bathroom but didn't make it. Maria managed to get a trash can in time to prevent him from making any more of a mess of the trailer than he already had.

"Fuck, you're crawling through glass. I'm calling an ambulance," Maria said.

He tried to stop her, but he was too sick and too dizzy. He could hear her talking, but the words didn't make sense. Collapsing next to the trash can, he wavered in and out of consciousness.

"I love her," he whispered again and again, hoping that if he continued to say it, something would change, and she would come running through the door to sweep him up.

Someone came running through the door, but it wasn't her. "What has he taken?"

"I don't know. The only thing I have found is this," Maria answered. He assumed she was holding up one of the bottles he had guzzled, but he wasn't able to actually check.

"Does he have any kind of history of this?" the stranger asked next.

"No, his vices are usually smoking cigarettes and sex. Don't think either would do this to him," Maria answered.

"Does he take any kind of prescription drugs?" they asked next.

"I'm not on fucking drugs!" he screamed, flinging his arm out and hitting someone who was near him. He hadn't realized anyone was there.

"Mr. Malcom, calm down. We are here to help," another voice he hadn't heard yet said. He tried to focus, tried to figure out what was happening to him, but he couldn't.

"He is a picture of health. Only pills I have ever seen him take are vitamins, and now and then, an aspirin," Maria answered.

"It's probably just alcohol poisoning. Depending on how full those bottles were, he could have way too much in his system. He also has several deep cuts. Let's get him in the ambulance. We will give him some oxygen, start an IV, and try to get some of the alcohol flushed out," the paramedic said. "Who is in charge of his health when he isn't capable?"

"I have all the paperwork for that. I can make decisions. Do you want me to go get it?" Maria answered.

"Yes please. We will get him moved and cleaned up," they answered. "Mr. Malcom, can you hear me?"

The voice sounded more distant, like it was under water, but he tried to answer. He wasn't sure if anything came out, though.

"Mr. Malcom, my name is Colt. I'm going to get you moved onto this stretcher. We are going to help you, okay?" the paramedic continued to explain.

They talked to him through the whole process, but he only heard bits and pieces through his battle with staying conscious. How long had he been out? It felt like he was swimming, but beneath it all was pain. Heavy drowning pain, and he wanted nothing to do with it. She had left. Naomi had left him.

Why did anyone ever fall in love? The pain of it was not worth the pleasure.

"Damion, I'm right here," Maria said, and he felt her take his hand. Maria would never leave him. She had been the only constant in his adult life.

"Mr. Malcom, I'm sorry, but we have to get that alcohol out of you," the parametric said.

The next few hours came in and out for him. They pumped his stomach and hooked him up to monitors and IVs. The whole time, Maria was there supporting him. At some point he completely passed out and was thankful for the reprieve into the darkness. The darkness was safe. Nothing could hurt him there.

It was dark outside the next time he opened his eyes. He was still in the back of the ambulance. Maria had probably told them not to take him to the hospital. Even in a crisis she would look out for his best interest. The media finding out that he had done this would be a shit show.

"Maria?" he groaned. His throat really hurt, and his body felt heavy.

"Damion?" she said and took his hand. It sounded like she had been crying.

"What happened?" he asked, not sure if what he remembered was reality or if he had imagined it all.

"Well, I think you drank a metric ton of vodka and then got really sick. Please tell me it was just the liquor. I don't have a drug problem to deal with now. Do I?" she asked, and he heard true concern in her voice.

"She left, Maria. She really left. Didn't she?" he asked, feeling the hot stab of his heart breaking once more.

"Damion, I don't really know what's going on. My priority is to make sure you're okay right now," Maria said.

"Don't worry. I'll be fine." He turned to look at her, knowing his words were a lie. He forced himself to smile and she leaned down and kissed the top of his head.

She stayed there, leaning against him and petted his hair like he was a child. Maybe he was in that moment. Maria was doing all she could to make him feel better, and while it wasn't doing much, the effort made him smile.

"Good to see you awake," a man said, stepping into the ambulance and taking a seat on the other side of the stretcher. "Do you remember anything that happened?"

"Not really," he answered.

"Well, I'm Colt. We found you in and out of consciousness. You had a lot to drink, and you had a lot of cuts. How are you feeling now?" the man asked.

Broken. The answer was broken, but that wasn't what the paramedic was asking. "I feel somewhat awake. Everything kinda hurts."

"Yeah, you will probably hurt for a little while. We got you patched up for the most part. I want to get another bag of fluids in you. We have a doctor on his way out. I think it is best to have you fully checked out before I release you. Okay?" Colt explained.

"Sure," Damion answered. It wasn't like he had anywhere he would rather be.

"I'm going to set you up in my trailer while we get yours cleaned up," Maria explained. He didn't care. He could have just slept on the ground by the trees for all he cared in that moment. Naomi was gone so nothing else mattered.

"Did Jessie call?" Damion asked.

"Yeah, she called a couple of times," Maria answered.

"Did you tell her?" he asked next hoping against all hope that Maria had kept her mouth shut on this.

"No, I didn't tell her about this. I just told her you couldn't come to the phone, and you would call her later," Maria answered, and Damion thanked whatever god may exist for that small favor.

The next question he almost had to force himself to ask, "And Naomi?"

"She hasn't called," Maria answered.

Tears filled his eyes, but he blinked them away. He refused to cry. It was his own fault for putting himself in that position. "I assume filming got canceled."

"Yeah, we all thought that was best. Not a lot of people actually know what happened, just that you are sick and needed some time off," Maria explained. She was good at her job, and he would always be thankful to her for that.

The doctor got there a few minutes later and asked Maria to wait outside the ambulance so the two of them could talk. "Well, Mr. Malcom, looks like you had a rough day."

"You could say that," Damion answered, not looking at the doctor. The older man took some time to give him a check over, flashing a light in his eyes and listening to his heartbeat. The man did let him know it was still beating. Damion was sure it had stopped completely.

"Your assistant said this is very outside of your normal behavior, but I have to ask, do you feel like you might hurt yourself?" the doctor asked.

Damion turned to look at the older gentleman. The name Dr. Turner was embroidered on his jacket, which was loose over his somewhat frail-looking body. The man was well past his prime based on the number of wrinkles on his face and the nearly white color of his slightly curly hair. Damion didn't really want to answer his questions, but he did because he knew it was the only way to make this all end so he could be alone.

"No, I'm not going to hurt myself. I wasn't trying to hurt myself to begin with."

"Well, I'm going to leave a card with your assistant for someone I know who is very good and very discreet. If you need to talk with someone, she would be trustworthy," the doctor explained. "Other than that, you seem to be pretty healthy. It seems you are past the danger at this point. You should probably avoid drinking for a couple of days. Other than that, you will heal up well. Just take it easy."

"I'll do my best," Damion answered.

It was another hour before they finally let him go. Maria brought him a pair of sweats to put on so he could leave the ambulance in some semblance of dignity. Apparently, the area had been completely blocked off, so no gawkers were waiting to catch a glimpse of him exiting the ambulance. He slowly walked with Maria to her trailer and stepped inside. He felt numb, which was better than before.

"You can take my bed. I'll sleep out here on the couch," Maria said, and when he started to protest, she just pointed for him to go back to the bed.

"Maria?" he asked, turning to look at her.

"Yeah?"

"Can you get me a pack of cigarettes?" Then went to bed.

CHAPTER THIRTY-FIVE

NAOMI

She hadn't gone home. Instead, she just drove and stayed at whatever RV park was available where she ended up. For the first couple of days, she completely ignored her phone, but she knew that was selfish of her. So after three days, she picked it up and called Jessie. She had so many missed calls that her voicemail was filled and no longer taking messages. Taking a deep breath, she prepared for Jessie to rip into her for ignoring her.

"It is about fucking time! Don't you know you can't make a pregnant woman worry like this?" Jessie said, picking up after three rings.

"Sorry about that," Naomi whispered. She hadn't slept since leaving Damion, and any time she thought she might, she freaked out and pushed through it. She was beyond exhausted and wondered how she had lived like that for so long.

"I would say it's okay, but it's not. What happened?" Jessie asked, her voice calming some. Her friend had been seriously worried.

"I don't know. I'm afraid, and I'm not ready for whatever is going on with me and Damion. It's only going to get harder," Naomi said, but she wasn't sure that was really the answer.

"That is a crock of shit. You are running away because you're scared? Is this still about Paul?" Jessie asked, and Naomi could hear the anger in her friend's voice.

"I feel like I'm losing him. I can't do that. I just can't," Naomi pleaded. She should have told Jessie about the dream. If she had told Jessie when it happened, her friend would better understand what was going on with her.

"Paul's dead! I know you don't want to accept it, but that is the truth. He is dead and not coming back. You can't cling to him when you have a hot-blooded man who actually loves you and wants to be with you," Jessie yelled from the other side of the phone.

"I know he's dead. Believe me. I am well aware of that fact. But if I lose his memory, what will I have?" Naomi cried.

"Naomi, you will never lose the memory of him. I keep telling you that, but you are so busy clinging on to him that you are missing the rest of your life. Paul would be so angry with you right now. I'm angry with you," Jessie said and then made a hissing noise.

Suddenly, Naomi's problems didn't matter. "Jessie? Are you okay?"

"Yes, I'm fine. Just been having some pain. I have an appointment with the doctor in two days. They said it's normal," Jessie answered.

"I'm coming home. I will be there tomorrow, okay," Naomi said. She could deal with her issues with Damion later. Jessie didn't sound good, and she had been so focused on her own mess that she hadn't realized the struggle Jessie seemed to be having.

"You really should go back to Damion and deal with that. I'm fine. I promise," Jessie said, but her breathing was heavy.

"I can deal with Damion later. I'm coming home," Naomi insisted.

The adrenaline woke her back up, and she got into the driver's seat. She had made it almost to Mississippi, so it would take her over a day to get back to Georgia. Naomi planned to be there when Jessie went back to the doctor.

Naomi sat next to Jessie as she waited hooked to a machine that was measuring contractions. It was far too early for her to be going into labor, but the doctor was concerned and wanted to get an idea of what was going on. He had hooked her up to a machine and was giving her fluids. Jessie hadn't put on enough weight, either, which was unlike her. Jessie had always been a little plump, so food had never been an issue for her.

Brad was at work, so Naomi was filling in for him where she could. When she got back into town, she had parked in front of Jessie's house, and she had been staying with them ever since. They didn't talk about Damion because they knew it would make them argue. Instead, they kept their focus on Jessie and the baby.

A knock sounded on the door, and a moment later the doctor walked in. He was looking at a clip board but looked up and smiled at the two of them. "Well, Mrs. Long, I would be lying if I said I wasn't concerned. The baby's heart rate is too high, and your blood pressure is too. You are showing signs of contractions. From now on you need to be completely in bed. Find a place in your house you don't mind being because the only time I want you up is to go to the bathroom."

"Is the baby going to come early?" Jessie asked, her eyes becoming glassy with tears.

"I'm going to give you some medication that will hopefully stop the contractions. We will keep monitoring everything, but please, no stress and no getting up and moving around. We want to keep that little bun in the oven as long as we can," the doctor answered.

"We were going to do a shower this weekend. Is that still a good idea?" Naomi asked next. They hadn't planned anything big. It was just going to be a few friends from school and people Brad worked with.

"So long as Jessie stays in a chair with her feet up the whole time, it should be fine. If you feel the pains getting worse, especially up your back, come into the hospital right away. Of course, if you show any other signs of labor, like your water breaking, come into the hospital right away. In cases like yours, we don't want you risking waiting it out," the doctor explained. "Do you have any other questions?"

"No, but I will call if anything comes up. Thank you for everything," Jessie said.

Naomi leaned over and hugged her friend. She was sure this was not the news she had wanted to hear. It made Naomi glad she was there. If anything happened to Jessie or the baby, Naomi would never forgive herself if she wasn't there to help.

A nurse came in, gave Jessie some medication, and then had her get into a wheelchair so she could be taken to the car. Jessie was not going to be happy stuck in bed, but Naomi would do her best to make the most of it. She would set up movie marathons and play games with her friend to keep her distracted.

"Naomi?" Jessie said once they were in the car.

"Yeah?" Naomi asked, turning the air on full blast to rid the car of the heat.

"I'm glad you're here. I didn't think I would need you so much right now, but I do. Just, don't forget that I'm mad at you about Damion, and we will be discussing it."

"After the baby is born you can yell at me all you want. For now, you don't need to stress about anything. I'm going to get some cards and such so we can keep you busy without you having to get up," Naomi explained.

After the car was in gear she reached over and squeezed her friend's hand. Jessie would get through this. She had worked too hard to have a child to let something like this stop it from happening.

CHAPTER THIRTY-SIX

DAMION

For two weeks he wallowed in his own self-pity while the movie wrapped up shooting, but now that it was done, he realized he was being an idiot. Naomi was afraid of getting close to someone, and in reality, he knew exactly how that felt. He had spent his entire life keeping people at arm's length so he wouldn't get close to them. Naomi on the other hand had given her all to someone and lost them. That was a pain he had never felt. It was selfish of him to be angry about it.

So instead he sat in his doctor's office. Most of Naomi's fear was connected to losing Paul. She was afraid of forgetting him, and she was afraid of losing someone like that again. Jessie had told him that no one knew Paul was at risk until it was too late. While Damion had never had any medical problems, Naomi's experience had been eye-opening. So there he sat waiting to tell his doctor that he wanted to know everything possible about his health.

Dr. Crawford walked into the room and smiled at him. He had been Damion's doctor for a long time, and they had developed a very good relationship over the years. "Hey, so what brings you in?"

"It is kinda complicated," Damion said, shifting on the little table he had been instructed to sit on.

"Well, I'm a doctor, so complicated is in the job descriptions," Dr. Crawford said.

Damion went about explaining the experience Naomi had with Paul, or at least what he knew about it. He didn't have all of the details, but he knew enough to give the doctor an idea of his train of thought.

"Doc, I'm in love with this girl, so I want to be able to show her that I'm not going to just randomly drop dead on her for no reason."

"So, you want me to just run a bunch of random tests on you without any medical need for them just so you can make sure you are as healthy as you are?" the doctor asked.

"Paul was healthy, from what everyone says, and it turned out he had that blood thing going on," Damion pointed out.

"That is very rare. Your friend just was a victim of a very unlucky tragedy. In all my years of being a doctor I have never seen or heard of a case like that. Doing all these tests can be extremely expensive, especially since there is no actual reason for it," Dr. Crawford explained.

"I'm aware, but I'll pay it. Poke, prod, and scan me until you know everything. I don't want to go back to her and fix things without this information," Damion explained.

"This goes against my better judgment, but if you really want to, and you're willing to pay for it, I'll order it all," he answered.

Dr. Crawfords's office quickly scheduled all the appointments, and over the next couple of weeks Damion went through a grueling series of test. He had no idea just how much was out there, and the bills were high. However, when the results were handed over to him, and he had a full clean bill of health, he knew it was worth it. He could go back to Naomi with the knowledge as a benefit in his direction. He couldn't give up on her, no matter how much she had hurt him by leaving.

He was on his way back to his car when his phone rang. Jessie's number flashed on his screen, and he picked it up. He hadn't told Jessie about his brief mishap with the vodka, not wanting to worry her. Since Naomi left, he hadn't really talked to Jessie again, so seeing her call made him curious. Maybe she had news about Naomi.

"Hey, Jessie, how is the baby coming?" he asked not wanting to make things all about him.

"Hey, Damion, this is Brad," a male voice said. Damion had met Brad on several occasions, but he had never called him before.

"What's up? Is everything okay?" Damion asked, leaning against the side of his car.

"Jessie is in the hospital. She would kill me for calling you, but I thought you would want to know. The baby is coming early. I know you two are close," Brad explained.

Worry flooded Damion. Jessie had become one of his best friends over the years. If she was in trouble, he wanted to be there for her. He was already back in LA, so he would have to catch a flight into Atlanta and then a car to the smaller town Jessie lived in. "I'm on my way. I'll be there as soon as I can."

"Thanks, man. I'm not going to bullshit and tell you not to come. I really think you should."

Damion was thankful the man hadn't tried to change his mind. He got in his car and started speeding toward his house. Once on the road, he called Maria so they could get travel arranged. Maria got straight to work while Damion frantically packed. He just threw things into a duffel bag hoping he got everything he would need. If not, he would buy it there. However, he made sure to grab one more thing.

Naomi had left a necklace in his bathroom, and he had only found it after she left. The necklace had an engagement ring on it, and he knew instantly it was Paul's ring. He had seen it before the two of them had started their romantic relationship and hadn't thought about the fact he hadn't seen it again. Grabbing the necklace, he shoved it into his bag before racing out of his apartment. There was no doubt he would run into Naomi if Jessie was in the hospital.

The airport was chaotic as always, but Maria managed to get him on the next flight out of LAX and to Atlanta. "A driver will be waiting for you. Get the information for the hospital Jessie is in, and they will route you. I will also call ahead and make sure you can get in without causing a scene. I'm sure the last thing Jessie will want is for your fans to take over the place," Maria said.

"You're the best," he said, hanging up and weaving his way through the airport. With the rush, he had no time to waste getting through security. As it was, he would be barely on time.

The flight was over four hours, and it took another three hours to get to the hospital from the airport. Damion was exhausted from the trip, but he wasn't going to go to the hotel first. Brad hadn't given him an update, so as he pulled up, he called.

"Hey, I'm pulling up now," Damion said, and the car pulled into the parking garage. He had been told to go to a service entrance.

"Good, I will come get you. They told me where you were going to be coming in. I will let them know you are here too," Brad answered.

"How is Jessie?" Damion asked.

"She is okay but freaked out. They have done all they could to stop the labor. I'll explain more when I get there," Brad said and hung up the phone.

It only took Brad a few minutes to get to the door, and he held it for Damion. At least Damion had packed an oversized hoodie. He lifted it to hide his face as they weaved through the hospital to the labor and delivery department. Brad explained that it was almost time for Jessie to give birth, and he had to get back as fast as possible.

"You didn't have to come get me," Damion said as he turned the corner to where Jessie's room would be.

"The other option would have been too awkward. You can wait in there, I have to go get to Jessie," Brad explained.

Damion wasn't sure what Brad meant by that, but he shook it off as frantic hysteria from his wife being in a medical emergency. With a deep breath, Damion turned and went into the room, stopping as he saw Naomi sitting in a chair by the window.

CHAPTER THIRTY-SEVEN

NAOMI

Her breath caught as she watched Damion walk into the room and remove the hood from his head. She had not expected to see him. How did he even know? Jessie had been so panicked that there was no way that she had called him. Had Brad?

Neither of them spoke. He looked at her, and she looked at him. Then he came and sat down in the chair next to hers. He leaned forward, resting his elbows on his knees and cradling his head in his hands. Jessie meant a lot to him for him to have dropped everything to come see her. Maybe he loved more than he let on.

Hours went by and still no word on what was happening. "I'm going to get some coffee," Naomi finally whispered, breaking the silence between them.

"Would you mind getting me one, too? I'm trying not to get noticed," he said, glancing over to her.

"Of course. I'll be right back," Naomi answered and got up to head for the coffee pot. The nurses had told them they could get some at any time. They kept it made.

She poured them both a cup, fixing it up how they liked before going back to the room. She should apologize to him. She should explain herself, but where was she even supposed to begin. With everything going on with Jessie, she hadn't even had time to think about her drama with Damion. He had been sitting so close to her that she could feel his warmth and smell the scent of his sandalwood soap. It stirred up all those good memories before she had gone and ruined everything.

When she walked into the room, Damion looked up at her and held his hand out. She was shaking as she handed over the hot cup but luckily managed not to spill anything. Once again, they fell into uncomfortable silence. The time ticked on so slowly that each minute felt like hours, but finally after what felt like an eternity Brad walked into the room.

He looked exhausted, but slowly a smile spread over his lips. "He's here. They are going to have to put him in one of those special beds, but he is here, and the doctor thinks he will be okay."

"That's good," Naomi and Damion said at the same time. They traded a look and then Naomi continued. "What about Jessie?"

"She's doing well. They are getting her fixed back up and then she will be moved back into here.

Damion stood up and walked over to Brad, giving him a big hug. "Congratulations, man. Everything is going to be fine. We will make sure of it."

"I'm glad you came. Jessie will be happy to see you," Brad said.

"I'll wait to see Jessie then go and try to find a place to stay," Damion said next.

"No, man, you can stay at our place. We have plenty of room, and there is no reason for you to get a room and be away from everything.

Besides, Jessie and I are going to be in the hospital for a while. It will be nice having people there to keep up with the place.

"Oh, I thought Naomi was there," Damion said, not looking back to her.

"I am there, but so is my RV. There really is plenty of room," Naomi said, getting up to give Brad a hug as well.

"Then it's settled. You stay at my house, and me and Jessie will be here," Brad said with a sense of finality.

They had put on all of the protective clothing, but the nurses were letting Jessie and Naomi in to see the baby. Jessie was doing a lot better than Naomi had thought she would be. It was a good sign. Jessie led the way to the incubator, and she was able to reach inside and hold the baby's hand. It was so tiny, much smaller than Naomi had thought he would be. He had been born too early to go home, but the doctors felt he was developed enough to be out of any true danger. It was good they were in a hospital and hadn't tried to do a home birth.

"He's beautiful," Naomi said, leaning her head on Jessie's shoulder.

"Yes, he is. We will have to stay a few weeks in the hospital, but everything should be okay," Jessie said. She turned to look at Naomi. "We named him Paul."

Naomi couldn't fight the tears that welled up in her eyes. The whole ordeal had already been emotional, but Jessie's words made it difficult to fight the tears. "He would have been so honored."

"Yeah, he would have loved him so much, just like I know you will," Jessie said. "See, he will never leave you. I promise. After all of this, don't you see how silly you are being. There are so many more important things in the world. It hasn't stopped, and you can't either. Fix this. Do it for him," Jessie said, nodding toward her child.

Naomi looked down at the tiny creature and smiled. Little Paul. Even early, there could not have been a more perfect baby in all the world. He wasn't even her son, but Naomi knew she would do anything and everything for the boy. "You're right. I need to take care of something first, though. Okay?"

"Yeah, you know I'm not going anywhere," Jessie said.

They stayed in there with Paul for a little longer before she was asked to leave while the doctors checked him. Naomi stood outside the window and watched as Jessie talked with the doctor before turning back to her son. Paul. She had named the little guy after Paul.

Passing Brad in the hall, she stopped him for a second. "I'm going to the cemetery," she told him and gave him a hug. "You guys picked a perfect name for him."

"We did. Jessie wanted to be the one to tell you, but we picked it out as soon as we knew we were having a boy. Paul Malcom Long. He has a lot to live up to," Brad answered. "You coming back to the hospital after you go to the cemetery?"

"No, I think I will go home for a bit and check on everything, but call me if you need me for anything," she answered. "I figure you and Jessie need some time together."

"Yeah, I just gave Damion the address to the house and a key to get in. Everything going to be okay?" Brad asked.

"Yeah, I think so. I just need to do something first," Naomi answered and gave Brad another hug.

She didn't stop by to tell Damion she was leaving. He would figure it out. Instead, she headed down to her car and drove off toward the cemetery. It had been raining the day Paul was put in the ground. She remembered it just like it was yesterday. The pain had been unbearable. Since then, she visited often, and until that year she'd always gone on the anniversary of his death and his birthday without fail. Working for Damion had kept her from being able to visit that year. It was strange.

Naomi parked and got out of the car, taking her time to walk and enjoy the day. Unlike the day of his funeral, today was sunny and warm. The humidity was dense, which made it hard to breathe, but other than that, it was a perfect day. She took her time walking along the path and green grass. When she got to the plot where Paul was buried, she sat down in the grass next to him.

"Jessie had her baby," she said, talking to the ground as if she were talking to him. "He is a perfect little boy but was born a little too soon, so he has to stay in the hospital. They named him after you. Well, you and Damion, which is very sweet. Paul, I don't know what I'm doing. I have been lost since the day you left me, but I think I really screwed things up lately. Jessie says I'm being stupid. She says I'm using you as an excuse not to be happy, and I'm starting to think she's right. I'm so afraid that if I give myself to someone else, I will forget you, and you were too important to me for that to happen. Is that stupid?"

She knew he wasn't going to answer, but she asked the question anyway and gave some time before she continued. "I think I'm in love with someone else. Five years have gone by, and I finally opened myself up to someone. I think you would like him. He is caring and funny. He isn't super serious and knows how to have fun. When I'm with him, I feel alive again. I think a part of me died with you that day, and until recently I was just a walking zombie, but Damion woke me up.

Well, actually, he let me sleep. It was amazing to finally get some rest and peace."

Naomi took a deep breath and sat there for a few minutes. The sun felt good on her skin, and she ran her fingers over the grass that had grown over Paul's grave. "I will always love you, and I will never forget you. You will be a part of my heart and soul until the day I die. When I do, I know I will see you in heaven and I hope you are proud of me when I get there. But everyone is right. It is time for me to move on. I hurt Damion. I know I did, and I have to make it right. Please understand that I'm not giving you up, I'm just adding someone to my life who can live with me."

She kissed her fingers and then reached out and touched them to his headstone. Tears filled her eyes, and she sat there letting them fall, but she didn't hurt. A soft breeze brushed over her cheek, and somehow she knew that was Paul's way of telling her it would all be okay.

She heard a rustling noise behind her and turned to see Damion standing there. He had his hands in his pockets and the most serious look she had ever seen. He wasn't looking at her. He was looking at Paul's headstone. How long had he been there? Had he heard what she said to him?

"Naomi, do you mind if I talk to Paul for a minute? Just the two of us?" Damion asked. It was not what she expected to hear him say, and it caught her off guard.

"Ummm, sure," she answered and stood up. She walked away from the grave area and watched as Damion knelt down. She tried to give him enough space, but she could still hear. Maybe he wanted to her to hear.

"Hey, Paul, so you don't know me. I'm Damion. I've been friends with Jessie for several years. She works for me but couldn't this year, so she sent me Naomi in her place. Look, I'm not sure I will ever be a perfect man, but I want you to know that I am going to do everything I can for the rest of my life to be as perfect as I can for Naomi. Even if she won't have me. I love her, but I know part of her heart will always belong to you. I would never change that. I would never want to take your place. I just want to pick up where you left off and take care of her. I hope you are cool with that," he said and then patted the ground.

As if on cue, like the universe giving Paul a voice, the nearly clear sky let loose a rainstorm. The sun was still shining but the sparse clouds had broken, and the rain fell upon them. She couldn't help it. Laughter burst out from her lips, and she began to spin around as the water soaked her through. When she looked over to Damion, he was smiling and laughing too. All the tension, all the pain, it washed away in that moment. Paul was telling them that he was okay with them, and that was all Naomi needed.

Damion seemed to understand the symbolism and marched over to her. His arms wrapped around her, and he lifted her to wrap around him as he kissed her breath away.

CHAPTER THIRTY-EIGHT

NAOMI

They sat on Jessie's couch, watching movies and snuggling. Part of her wanted to just jump back into things, but rushing seemed like the wrong idea. So instead, they relaxed and enjoyed the relief the day had brought them. Jessie and baby Paul were safe and healthy, and the two of them could work past all of these demons Naomi had let control their relationship.

When the credits rolled on the movie they had been watching, Damion reached over and clicked off the TV. "We need to talk," he said and took her hands.

"I figured that," Naomi answered. "Do you want to start?"

"Yes," he said. "First, I want you to know that when you left, it was probably the hardest thing I ever went through. I did some stupid shit, but I'm fine now."

"What do you mean you did some stupid shit?" Naomi asked, concern in her eyes.

"I finished off that bottle of vodka within seconds and then drank another and ended up in an ambulance with alcohol poisoning, but after that I didn't do anything else bad. I was angry and sad and heartbroken for a few weeks. I smoked several cartons of cigarettes, and then woke up one day and realized I was being an idiot," he explained.

"I'm sorry I did that to you," she whispered.

"No, it's fine. I mean, it doesn't matter anymore. Look, I realized that you were afraid for something that I couldn't even begin to understand. I will never pretend to understand what you went through. God, I hope I never have to know what that felt like, but I did want to do something for you," he said then stood up and went to his bag. He pulled out a packet of papers and handed them to her. "I went to my doctor and told him I wanted to be tested for anything and everything that might possibly cause what happened to Paul to happen to me. I told him that I wanted to be able to come to you with certainty that if anything happened to me, we would either know ahead of time or it would truly be an accident."

"Are you serious?" Naomi asked, opening the packet to see stacks of paperwork for various tests. "You did this for me? It had to have cost a fortune."

"Yes, I did it for you, and I don't care how much it cost. You can look through all of it if you want to, but I can tell you, he found nothing. There aren't even signs that my lungs are bad from smoking, though I have been working on officially quitting. It hasn't been easy. I've been smoking since I was a teenager," he answered, sitting back down next to her. "My doctor thought I was insane, and he said what happened to you was a really rare thing, but I had to do it. I had to make sure you knew where things stood with me. I have a one hundred percent clean bill of health, and I will make sure I go to the doctor regularly and keep it that way."

She didn't know what to say. He had gone above and beyond what anyone should ever do, and he had done it all for her. Naomi set the papers down on the coffee table and then wrapped her arms around him. She held him close to her, feeling his warmth and breathing him in as little pieces of her heart started to heal.

"I agree with your doctor. You are insane, but I couldn't be more thankful."

"I know," he whispered and reached into his pocket. "I know the other thing you were afraid of was that you would forget Paul. I'm not going to let that happen, no matter what." He held out his hand to show her that he had found her necklace with Paul's ring.

Naomi had panicked when she realized it was missing but had been in the middle of everything with Jessie, so she hadn't had a chance to do anything about it. "Where did you get this?"

"You apparently left it in my bathroom one night. I'm not sure when, but I found it when I was packing up my trailer. I wanted to make sure you had it, and you can wear it if you want. It doesn't bother me. I know that he comes as part of who you are," Damion answered.

"This means more to me than I can even say," Naomi said and then put on the necklace. "Look Damion, I can't promise that things with me won't still be hard. I'm probably still going to have bad days, but I'm going to try. I don't want to be alone anymore.

Damion smiled and then crashed his lips to hers. The kiss was savage and hungry, and she got swept up in it. When he broke from it, he almost growled, "You better point me in the direction of a bedroom or I'm going to take you on the floor right now."

Heat swept over her body as she stood up and took his hand, leading him to the room she had been staying in. The moment they were inside the room, he returned to kissing her. His strong hands didn't just remove her clothes, he ripped them from her, leaving the tattered fabric in the wake of their movements toward the bed.

She wasn't as strong, so all she managed to do was unsnap and un-button things before she fell back onto the bed. He stripped so quickly she thought he had managed to get superpowers. He crawled onto the bed and was inside her within seconds. They kissed as their hands roamed all over each other. His body moved in hard fast motions to build her up as fast as possible. It wasn't sweet love making. It was hard savage taking. She knew this was deeper than the physical actions. Damion was claiming her, body and soul.

Her first orgasm was almost painful as it tore through her, and she screamed out into the darkness of the room. She pushed at him and rolled them over so she could take control. It was her turn to put her stamp on him. She rode him savagely with all the carnal intensity the moment asked for. She bent over, licking and biting along his heated flesh as his hands gripped her ass, guiding her movements. Then it was as if they both fell into it at the same time. He called out her name as he arched deeply into her, his head flung back and his fingers bruising her as he shook and writhed below her. Every vibrating spasm of her own orgasm burst through each and every nerve in her body until she became a vessel of pleasure.

The two of them collapsed. "I love you," she whispered into his chest. She could feel even more tension leave him.

"I love you, too," he answered, leaning up a bit to kiss her softly.

Naomi didn't even shift off of him, lulled to sleep by the pounding of his heart. His fingers lightly traced up and down on her spine, and she knew she was home. Damion had become her home, and she didn't want to go another day without him.

Brad had come home for a shower and a decent meal, so Naomi cooked up a large breakfast. Her body was aching from her night of marathon sex with Damion, but it was the blissful pain that came from being with someone who mattered. She would savor every moment of it.

Damion and Brad were casually chatting at the table while sipping coffee and laughing over various things. Brad had his phone out and was showing them a million pictures of baby Paul. The man was the proudest papa in the world, and Jessie was lucky to have him in her life.

"Oh, you should have seen it. He was making all these little faces. The nurses said it was all gas, but I refuse to believe it. My boy was happy and smiling every time Jessie reached in there to take his hand. God I can't wait to be able to bring him home."

Naomi smiled as she set a couple of plates down. She had made omelets, bacon, fruit, and biscuits. She arched a brow at Damion, letting him know the war was not over. Damion looked back and forth between her and the offending bread on his plate. An odd expression crossed his face, and to her surprise, he picked up the biscuit and took a bite. She almost laughed at the look that came over his face. A moan left his throat, and she had to hide the shiver the sound caused her.

"Holy fuck what is wrong with me. I've been saying no to this?" Damion said and took another bite.

"Oh, Naomi's biscuits are famous. My work would have me bring some in when we were having company breakfast. I have no idea how she does it, but she can make the healthiest stuff taste like you are committing food sin," Brad said, slicing open his own biscuit to add a healthy scoop of jelly.

"I'm such a foolish man. I should have given in to this months ago," Damion said again. "You win." He winked at her, and Naomi burst out laughing. She was going to have to find something else for the two of them to argue over now. Taking a seat, she joined in on breakfast and enjoyed the company. She hadn't been happy in so long that finding it felt like such a relief that it was seamless.

CHAPTER THIRTY-NINE

DAMION

Jessie was coming home, and he and Naomi had spent the last two days getting the house ready. It had been a month, but the doctors had finally cleared Paul to leave the hospital. They were going to have to be careful for a while, and Jessie had said she wouldn't be taking him out in public until he was a bit stronger, but Damion knew his friend was more than ready to come home.

He was hanging a welcome home sign while Naomi went around setting balloons and streamers everywhere. They were making a big deal out of the homecoming and had even put balloons on the street sign and mailbox. Everyone in the neighborhood was going to know that baby Paul was coming home.

"They're here," Naomi said, coming over and swatting him a bit. She was so excited, and he loved seeing the look on her face.

"One more second. I almost got it." He groaned. "Being tall doesn't mean I can automatically do all the high stuff."

"Yes, it does," Naomi teased.

Finally getting the push pin to go into the wall, he turned around just in time for Brad to throw the door open. "Welcome home!" he and Naomi said at the same time.

Jessie laughed and slowly walked in with Paul nestled in her arms. She was looking good and had even lost a lot of the baby weight already. Her hair was piled on her head in a fiery messy bun, but at least there was color to her skin. He had been worried about her, so seeing her healthy did a lot to ease his concerns.

"You guys didn't have to do all of this. Paul isn't going to remember any of it." Jessie laughed, coming over and giving both of them hugs.

"We did it for you," Naomi answered.

"You wanna hold him?" Jessie asked with a beautiful smile spreading over her lips.

"Oh, yes, please!" Naomi said excitedly.

The two ladies exchanged the child and Damion was not prepared. Seeing Naomi there holding the baby in her arms suddenly did things to him he had not expected. She would be a wonderful mother, and he wanted her to be the mother of his children.

"He's gotten bigger," Damion said, reaching over and brushing a bit of Paul's reddish-brown hair from his forehead.

"Yeah, he's almost eight pounds now. He is our little fighter," Jessie answered.

"Hey, Paul, it is nice to meet you. I'm going to be your uncle Damion, even though we aren't actually related. You will still be my family. I'm going to take you to all the movies you want and spoil you rotten," he whispered, and Naomi motioned for him to take the child.

Damion had never held a baby before, so he was nervous as he took Paul into his arms.

"Damion Malcom, you will not get my child into any trouble, or I will beat your ass," Jessie said.

"Language, woman, there are innocent ears present," Damion teased and then turned his attention back to the boy. "Don't worry. If you don't tell, I won't tell either."

"Oh, you are impossible. Do you hear this, Brad?" Jessie protested, going over to her husband for backup.

Apparently, Brad was upholding the bro code because he just laughed. "I have no idea what you are talking about."

"Naomi, what are we going to do? These men are the worst." Jessie laughed and went to sit on the couch.

Damion passed Paul back to Naomi, who went to sit with Jessie on the couch, "Oh they are just all talk."

"True, besides, my boy is going to know not to mess with his momma or face the wrath," Jessie said laughing.

It was a beautiful homecoming, but as Damion stood there watching the ladies on the couch, he realized the time had come. Everything was clear.

He had made reservations at the nicest restaurant in town. It wasn't as fancy as a place in LA or New York like he would have usually taken Naomi to, but it was the best the town had to offer. Damion had let Naomi know that he wanted to take her out somewhere nice and give Jessie and Brad some privacy.

He held her hand as he led her into the restaurant, and they were seated instantly. His heart was racing, but he had made up his mind. It might be the craziest thing he would ever do, but he couldn't wait any longer.

The waitress brought over some wine and bread, and then the two ordered their meals. He could barely hold himself together through dinner. Brad was the only one who knew of his plans and was in full support. When the plates for the entrees were removed, Damion took a deep breath.

"Naomi, I need to tell you something," he said, his mouth going dry like a desert was taking over where his tongue usually was.

"Okay?" a strange look crossed her face. He swore he saw her start to panic, but he couldn't stop. He had to get it out.

Moving around closer to her, he took her hand. "I love you. You are my one. I know I'm your two, but you are my one. I have never felt so strongly or been more sure of anything in my life."

"Damion, what are you saying?" Naomi asked.

He kicked back his chair and got down on one knee. A gasp spread through the restaurant, and he knew all eyes were on him. Oh, he hoped she said yes. It would kill him if she didn't. "You are the first thing I think of when I wake up and the last thing I think of when I go to sleep. I think I loved you the moment I first danced with you in the rain that drunken night, and the way you smiled at me is forever tattooed on my soul. I don't want to live another moment of my life if you aren't in it. So, here with all these witnesses and God, if you believe in that, I'm asking you. Naomi Grace Crestwood, will you marry me?"

His hands were shaking as he reached into his pocket and pulled out the ring he had purchased for her. He had actually bought two, but he pulled out the fancier more expensive one first. Opening the box, he held his breath as he waited for her to say something. Please say something.

Naomi lifted a hand to her lips and then reached out to look at the ring. The diamond was huge and of the highest quality. It was all platinum and sparkle and much more than she would ever actually want, but if she married him, she would need bling when they were at events together. "This is way too much."

"Yeah, I thought you might say that," he said and placed that box on the table. A buzzing energy permeated the air as the restaurant watched the show they were putting on. "So, I'll try again."

He pulled out another box and opened it. The ring inside was smaller. The diamond was still perfect, and everything was still of the highest quality, but this ring was more subtle, more fitting for the woman sitting before him. "Okay, Naomi Grace Crestwood, will you marry me?"

Again, the silence filled the air. After a few seconds someone from across the dining room called out. "Oh, come on, honey, put him out of his misery!"

Naomi laughed and light filled her eyes as she took his hand and with the sweetest sound answered. "Yes... yes, I will marry you."

The restaurant erupted in cheers as he reached out and pulled her to him, kissing her with every ounce of passion he possessed. He took the ring, slid it onto her hand, and then held her hand up to the room. "She said yes! I'm getting married!"

Tears of joy fell down Naomi's cheeks, and when he finally pulled his chair back to the table to sit down like a normal person she reached over and kissed his cheek. Her eyes went to the other box with the more expensive ring. "So why did you get two rings?"

"Well, I knew you weren't the kind of girl to want something too fancy, but I'm a movie star, and when we are out together in Hollywood you will need something fancy. This is your movie star ring. The one on your hand is the 'I understand you better than you think' ring," he answered. He closed the other box and put it back in his pocket.

"Oh, you think you know me so well. Do you?" she teased, leaning in and kissing him softly.

"I know I do. I talked it over with Paul," he said. "After all, I had to ask his permission."

"You did what?" she said, and tears started to form in her eyes.

"Well, I asked baby Paul too, but yeah. I went to the cemetery and asked Paul if it was okay. I'm not sure what the answer was but I didn't get struck down by lightning or anything, so I think it's cool," he answered.

He wanted her to know without a doubt that he would always be understanding of that part of her life. Her life with Paul had made her the woman she was with him. He would always be thankful for that.

Chapter Forty

Naomi

D amion and she stood in the cemetery together next to Paul's grave. He almost always came with her to visit, and if she asked for privacy, he gave it to her. However, it was a special day, and he was standing by her side. Most people would tell them it was bad luck. After all, the groom wasn't supposed to see the bride before the wedding, but she figured the universe would make an exception for this.

"Hi, Paul, we wanted to stop by and tell you that if you want you can come to the wedding. I know you would want to be there for me," Naomi said, reaching over and pressing her hand to the headstone. "I love you, and I still expect to see you on the other side."

"Yeah, and I want you to know I have every intention of taking care of her. So if for some reason you are restless, just know she is going to be fine, and you can go enjoy heaven," Damion said.

They stood there for a moment, and Naomi reached up to touch the ring hanging from her neck. Damion never got upset when she wore it. He was so understanding of the situation and had actually encouraged her to wear the ring to the wedding. It meant Paul would be with her, and that was everything to her.

After a couple of minutes, Damion pulled at her hand and motioned for her to follow him out. They had a wedding to get to, after all. Her dress was simple, soft white layers and a princess heart top with a bit of lace and beading. She had her hair done up with a few strands framing her face. She felt like a queen, and when Damion had seen her in her dress, he had almost ruined her makeup kissing her. As they walked down the path back to the limo, her skirt floated around her in the most beautiful way.

They got into the car and made their way to the venue. They had chosen to have an outdoor wedding in a lovely garden. It had been over a year since Damion asked her to marry him, but they had wanted to wait until after the movie premiere and for baby Paul to be in better health. He was thriving, and no one would ever have known he was premature.

The day was sunny and just cool enough to keep them from melting in the Georgia sun. The press had swarmed the outside of the garden, and they gave in to taking a few pictures for them before making their way inside. Maria was standing just on the other side of the door, dressed in a lovely pink dress.

"You two just can't do anything normal. Can you?" she said as she took Damion's hand to drag him to the altar. "Y'all should have been here an hour ago. People were starting to wonder if the two of you ran off."

"We had to make a stop first, but no, we aren't going to run away." Damion laughed, looking over his shoulder at her. He mouthed the words "I love you" to her before Maria had him out of sight.

Jessie walked over and helped adjust her dress. Naomi decided not to wear a veil since Damion was going to see her anyway. There was no point in hiding away from him.

"Oh, you look so beautiful. How have you managed this?" Jessie said, sniffing back tears.

"Don't you dare start crying. If you cry, I will cry, and it will all go downhill from there," Naomi said and then pulled Jessie in for a hug.

"I make no promises. Now, let's get you married before you do something stupid," she said.

Jessie passed a giant bouquet of lilies and roses to Naomi to hold and then took her own smaller version. Music started to play, and Jessie went through the small curtain that separated them from their guests. After another couple of seconds, the curtain was pulled open and the crowd stood as Naomi began her walk to the altar. There were hundreds of people, most of them were there for Damion, but Naomi's friends and family were there, too. She just had a lot less of them than he did.

However, the moment her eyes met his, everyone else disappeared. When she got to him, he held out his hand and took hers. She passed the flowers back to Jessie and turned to face the man who would be her husband in less than an hour. The whole ceremony went by in a blur. They didn't have a religious ceremony but a more casual one with words of love.

"You asked me once how I was able to make all these movies and show love when I didn't know what love was. I see now exactly what you meant. I never knew just how much I was leaving off of the screen. You showed me love, hope, and happiness the likes of which I never imagined. Before you, I had resigned myself to be alone the rest of my life. You changed that. You are my one, and I will eat your biscuits every day for the rest of my life," Damion said. Some people in the crowd laughed. Others seemed very confused, but if you knew you knew.

"I was lost when I met you. I was the broken shell of a person and thought I would never be whole again. You put my pieces back together. You put up with me when I'm having bad days. You hold me when I'm sad. You make me laugh, and you fill me with love every single day. I was sleepless before I met you. My body and soul falling more and more apart with every passing day. You gave me peace, helped me sleep and heal, and then showed me that I was worthy of love again. You may be my two, but you are the best two anyone could ever ask for, and for the rest of my life, you will be number one in my heart," she said.

The officiant went through the more traditional moments with rings and I dos, and then finally the moment came. "Ladies and Gentlemen, I would like to now present to you Mr. and Mrs. Crestwood Malcom!" the officiant called out. "You may kiss your bride."

Damion pulled her into him and kissed her as if no one was watching. They got lost in that moment for several minutes before Jessie told them to get a room. The crowd cheered, and they walked hand in hand back down the aisle. Before the wedding they had decided to combine names. He would still use Malcom in Hollywood because it was his brand, but they wanted their relationship equal.

They had just gotten under the catering tent where there would be dancing and food would be served when the lightest shower hit. It only lasted a couple of minutes before it passed, and Damion kissed her softly. She loved him, and he loved her. Nothing could be more perfect than that.

About the author

Vanessa Rose is a Contemporary Romance author currently residing in Tuscaloosa, Alabama. She can often be found at a coffeeshop working on her books and refers to these trips to town as "Going to the Office". She credits her friends and family with inspiring her and being a sound board as she plots out her next book. To read her Paranormal Romance works, look for her under the pen name Cherron Riser.

Facebook Group - https://www.facebook.com/groups/vanessaroseromancereads

Instagram – https://www.instagram.com/author_vanessa_rose/